Girl

in the

Woods

SUNCOAST PARANORMAL 4

by

Lovelyn Bettison

This is a work of fiction. Names and incidents are products of the author's imagination. Any resemblance to actual persons living or dead is entirely coincidental.

Nebulous Mooch Publishing

2021

Prologue

Stephanie stood on her front lawn, staring down the street to the end of her cul-de-sac where her piece of suburbia bumped up against the nature preserve. She was never a wilderness lover, and the idea of having coyotes, bobcats, panthers, and alligators as her neighbors terrified her. Sometimes, she swore she felt something watching her from the woods when she was outside weeding the flower beds. She hoped it wasn't a panther plotting to make her its next meal.

As she stood on her freshly manicured lawn enjoying the cool early morning air, a sense of dread settled into her. She saw a flash of red out of the corner of her eye, but when she turned to look, nothing was there. It must've been a cardinal.

The branches of the ancient trees at the end of the street danced in the wind, and beneath the sound of the rustling of leaves, she swore she heard a child laughing.

Someone was watching her. She could feel it. Longing for privacy and safety, she turned around to go inside and was stunned to see a little girl standing in front of her porch. The girl had a round face with plump cheeks and large doe eyes. She wore a red dress, the kind with a flouncy skirt and puffed sleeves. The collar was made of white eyelet. She wore a scuffed black mary-jane shoe on one foot, and the other was bare. The girl's chubby cheeks sagged a little. Her mousy hair was cut into a chin-length bob. In one hand, she held a teddy bear. Its fur was worn from love, and on its chest was an embroidered heart the same color as the girl's dress.

Upon seeing the girl, Stephanie jumped back. "Where did you come from?" Stephanie put on her kindest voice as she approached the child who blinked up at her silently.

Stephanie looked around, hoping to see who the girl was with, but there was no one else outside.

She was new to the area and still didn't know the neighbors. "Where are your parents? You can't be here alone." She looked down at the girl's bare foot. "Where's your other shoe?"

The girl didn't respond. She just continued to stare up at Stephanie, blinking slowly.

"Do you live around here?" She hadn't seen the girl before.

The girl remained silent.

Stephanie looked to the right, then to the left, wondering which neighbor's door she should knock on first. It was so early that the sun had only just begun to rise. "Let's go try to find your parents." She reached out her hand to the child, but before she could touch her, the child held her finger to her lips.

"You want me to be quiet. Why? Is this a game?"

The child smiled at the question before running around Stephanie and beckoning her to follow just before she ran up the path and disappeared from view.

"Wait!" Stephanie took off after her. She had thought of the forest as a place too dangerous for her, let alone a young child. Somehow the girl was fast. She ran into the woods and, despite her red dress, seemed to disappear among the trees.

"Where are you?" She yelled into the woods again and again, her heart pounding.

Stephanie trudged around among the trees, looking for the

child until the sun rose in the sky and her body was drenched in sweat. She needed to get to work. Convincing herself that the girl had probably gone home, she went home too.

When she walked up onto the front porch, she noticed the front door was ajar. She hadn't remembered leaving it that way, but it was possible. She'd only gone outside to get some fresh air and hadn't expected to leave the front yard. Her heart thumped at the thought of having been robbed, but the area was relatively safe. Not many people came around who didn't live there. That was one of the reasons she and her fiancé, Will, chose the neighborhood. She reminded herself of that as she went inside.

The house was untouched. Her cell phone sat on the kitchen table playing the podcast she'd been listening to. The smoothie she had made herself for breakfast waited for her on the kitchen counter. She could still make it to work on time. So she hurried through the house getting ready. She had to shower and change, put on her makeup, and do her hair. She was so busy getting ready that she almost didn't notice the stuffed bear with a red heart embroidered on its chest on her bed. The fur was worn away on its left arm, and it only had a single black button eye. She walked up to it and took it in her hand.

"Hello!?" she called. Had the girl been inside her house? Had she left it?

She searched every room, every closet, and under the bed only to find nothing.

Not knowing what to do, she set the bear on top of the dresser and went to work.

Later Stephanie would be able to point to this day as the day everything in her life began to go wrong.

Chapter 1

Day stood at the end of the driveway with her arms crossed over her chest when they pulled up. Her black hair was cut short, with a shock of gray in the front. She wore a pair of dark gray slacks and a loose-fitting green blouse tucked in at the waist. When Adam first met Day, he had no idea that she, like Cheryl, was a psychic. She seemed like the exact opposite of what he thought of when he thought of someone who told fortunes. She was straightlaced and carefully pulled together. She looked more like she was ready for a day at the office than a day exorcising ghosts and reading tarot. She carried herself with a calm elegance that reminded Adam of an old-time movie star. Before he even turned off the car, she was at the car window.

"Love the new car," she said to Adam. He was still driving the rental Toyota Camry while the insurance company figured out whether they would total his car. "How was your trip?"

Cheryl got out, arching her back and stretching like they really did come right to the house from their trip when in reality they had stopped off at home first, showered, changed, and even done some unpacking. "Long," Cheryl said. "I'm sure glad to be back."

Adam was glad to be back too. When they left, he'd known that what they were doing would be difficult, but he never expected it to end up the way that it had. Paranormal investigation was taxing. It was certainly much harder than freelance IT work, but it was something he felt called to do. It was turning him into a completely different person.

"I want to hear about everything that happened." Day hooked her arm in Cheryl's and led her into the house.

"I'll tell you about it soon," Cheryl said. "First, I want to know what's going on here."

Day and Cheryl fell into sync so quickly. Cheryl had only lived in St. Pete for a few years but had acquired the type of friendships that seemed like they'd started a lifetime ago. He always marveled at that because he had never been that good at having close friends. He followed them into the house, a white Mediterranean with a red tile roof on the edge of a nature preserve. When they stepped into the entryway, he noticed that the house still had an unlived-in feel even though its occupants, Stephanie and Will, had moved in a few weeks ago. Their footsteps echoed on the white tile floors as they walked into the living room. Stephanie and Will sat on the sofa. Moving boxes still waiting to be unpacked sat against the wall. Upon seeing them come in, Will got up and walked straight over to Adam, his hand extended to shake.

"How are you doing?" Will said, holding onto Adam's hand a few seconds too long.

"Good." Adam tried to pull his hand away, but Will tightened his grip and stepped in closer to him.

"You know I don't believe in any of this, but I'm willing to give it a go if it will make Steph feel better." He grimaced before releasing his hold on Adam. Will had square features. His strong jawline and dimpled chin reminded Adam of someone who should be anchoring the local news. There was something about how he talked that felt rehearsed, almost like he was reading from a script.

"We'll do anything we can to help." Adam smiled

reassuringly.

Stephanie was Cheryl's best friend. Over time, Adam had gotten to know her too. She had cycled through a lot of relationships that didn't work out and had experienced a lot of heartbreak. She deserved the best in life. Like Cheryl, he was committed to doing whatever he could to help her.

Stephanie got up from the couch and gave Cheryl a long hug. "I'm so glad you came." When she stepped away from Cheryl, she wiped a tear from her eye. "It's been so hard." She bit down on her bottom lip to stop the quivering. "I can't even explain."

Cheryl pushed the hair from Stephanie's forehead, a maternal gesture. "I'm sorry, but you're going to have to try. I need to hear everything so we can help you."

"Will and I will tell you what we know," Day said. "Stephanie can fill in the blanks when she feels comfortable."

Stephanie and Will settled cross-legged onto the floor, leaving the sofa to their guests. Will cleared his throat, "This is what I remember--"

"I can do it." Stephanie reached out and took his hand. "This has been happening to me, and I need to talk about it."

Adam sat forward on the sofa, leaning in to make sure he heard every detail of her story.

Chapter 2

Stephanie never thought she would leave St. Pete, but everything in her life was pushing her across the Skyway Bridge. She wanted something different, and even though she had gotten over her ex-boyfriend, living a few houses down from him was painful. Sometimes she would look out the window only to see him and his girlfriend walking their new puppy up the street and feel a pang of regret. Yes, time had passed. She had dated other guys and was with Will now, but she still wondered what her life would've been like with him. She needed to start over someplace else. When the job in Sarasota came through, it was a sign. Then Will proposed. There was no reason to hang on to her old life or her old house. It was time to let all of that go.

Stephanie pulled into the driveway behind the real estate agent's red Tesla. As soon as she had the house in her sights, she knew it was perfect. The white stucco Mediterranean with the red tile roof looked like a vacation villa she would stay in on a trip to Spain, if she had ever gone to Spain. A brick path ambled up to the porch with palm trees that look like upside-down feather duster's standing tall on either side. Three steps led up to the arched doorway. A heavy, black cast-iron knocker hung on the dark wooden door. Stephanie admired the house through her car window. She took a quick glance at herself in the rearview mirror, using her hand to smooth down any flyaways in her chestnut-colored hair and checking her lipstick for smudges. The real estate agent had already gotten out of her car and stood in the driveway, waiting.

"This is it," Stephanie said to herself before opening the car door and stepping out. She wished Will had come with her, so he could feel the magic that she was experiencing right now. She knew she should try to play it cool, but she couldn't help herself. "It's amazing," she said to the real estate agent as she shut her car door.

The agent, a thin woman in her early fifties with a striking platinum buzz cut, said, "You haven't even been inside yet." She hurried to the door and opened it, revealing an entryway with white tile and a tall ceiling featuring a small chandelier.

Stephanie couldn't help but gush. "This is exactly what I always dreamed of living in. It's just perfect."

She followed the real estate agent through the house and heard all about the square footage and the amenities of the neighborhood. She knew all of these things were important, but she only half paid attention because she had already made up her mind. Stephanie was a woman who knew what she wanted, and this house was exactly that.

Later she would admit that her enthusiasm for the style of the house clouded her judgment. Usually, she was someone who trusted her gut, but she wanted this home so badly that she ignored the way it made her feel.

It all felt too good to be true until she stepped out into the back garden. Sliding glass doors led from the living room into a narrow backyard surrounded by a wooden fence.

"The best thing about this house is that you have so much privacy. It sits right on the edge of the nature preserve where you can hike the trails and see the local wildlife. It's known for being a beautiful natural habitat right here in the middle of the suburbs." The real estate agent motioned to the canopy of oaks hanging overhead. Curtains of Spanish moss swayed from their thick branches.

Stephanie stood on the rectangular patio of carefully placed paving stones and looked out at the patch of soft bright green grass with the oak branches hanging overhead. It was a lovely scene. She could imagine her children playing out there one day. It was so easy to picture a future here, but something dark tugged at the place just beneath her solar plexus. It made her stomach rumble and bile rise in her throat. She swallowed hard, pushing the acidic taste down. "It's beautiful," she said weakly. The feeling pushed at her. A relentless darkness engulfed her, and for a moment, she felt as if she couldn't get oxygen into her lungs. Breathless, she turned and walked back inside. The echo of her hard-soled shoes on the tile seemed louder than before. The sound bounced painfully around in her skull. She put her hand to her forehead and closed her eyes.

The real estate agent stepped inside. "Are you okay?"

Stephanie shook her head. "I'm feeling a little bit sick. Just give me a minute." She took some slow, deep breaths, trying her best to push out whatever had crawled inside her. She had learned that breathing deeply was often all she needed to do to quell her anxiety. As she inhaled the stale air, the anxiety and darkness rushed out. "I'm feeling better already."

"Good." The real estate agent looked down at her phone. "I have a couple more places I want to show you if you have time."

"I don't need to see any other places," Stephanie said. "I want to show Will this house and then hopefully"--she crossed her fingers--"put an offer on it. Do you know if anyone else has put an offer on it recently?"

"It's just gone up on the market. You're one of the first people to see it. I don't know how long it will stick around though. It is a really good price. If you want to put an offer on it, you need to do it right away. Can you get Will here to see it today?"

"Yes, I'm pretty sure I can get him to come take a look at it." She was already deciding what color she would paint the living room walls.

**

Stephanie was surprised when they actually got the house. She had to talk Will into buying it. He was reluctant at first but relented when he realized how important it was to her. Stephanie was sure they would end up in a bidding war, but somehow they'd managed to snap up the property before anyone realized what a steal it was. When they closed on the place, they'd made love on the kitchen island as soon as they got the keys. They finally had a home together. Will had decided to buy a house with her. They were both on the mortgage, and it felt like the biggest commitment a man had ever made to her. The house made the fact that they were engaged more real than anything. There was no backing out. They were in this together. Will was smart, funny, and complicated, and he was going to be her husband.

She'd been looking for someone to commit to life with her like that for so long that she almost stopped believing it was possible, and now here it was. With a new house and a new job, Stephanie was ready to walk into her bright new future.

From the first night she spent in the house, Stephanie stopped dreaming. Her sleep was dark and heavy. Waking up felt more like coming out of an anesthesia-induced slumber than a restful sleep. She met the morning with a dull headache that settled in the center of her forehead.

"Are you okay?" Will leaned against the kitchen counter,

holding a stainless-steel travel cup of coffee.

Stephanie sat at the round oak table with her head in her hands. "Yeah, it's just a headache."

"You should go to the doctor about that. You've been getting them all the time." He picked his keys up from the counter. "Are you okay to go to work?"

"I just started. I have to go whether or not I'm okay." Stephanie's new job had been harder than she anticipated. There were so many things to learn, but she was up for the challenge. When she felt stuck or frustrated, she would remind herself that struggling through the steep learning curve would be better for her in the long run. "I'll be fine. I took a Tylenol. I'm just waiting for it to kick in."

"All right, then. I have to head out." He walked over to her and kissed her on the forehead before leaving.

She listened to his car start and back out of the driveway. She didn't want to go to work, but she had to. She looked up at the clock on the stove, only fifteen minutes before she needed to leave. Hopefully, her painkillers would start working by then. She sat on the hard wooden chair, trying not to think about her headache. Even when her head hurt, all she had to do was look around the empty slate that was her house, and her heart would begin to leap with joy. Once things slowed down with her new job, she would have time to start decorating. Until then a lot of their belongings remained in boxes. Their furniture was a conglomeration of what both of them had previously owned. It didn't match. Will favored black and gray furniture with sharp edges and leather sofas. Her taste had been warmer, rounder, and involved a lot of rattan. She was going to make it work though. She just needed time to get started.

Stephanie was focusing on not having a headache when she noticed the sound of the birds twittering in the treetops had grown a bit louder. She looked up to see a squirrel scamper across the floor. It stopped at the entrance to the hallway and sat up on its haunches. Stephanie shot up out of her chair. Her first instinct was to jump on the table and screech with fear, but she was the only one there. If she didn't want her house to be infested with squirrels, she needed to figure out where this one came from and how to get rid of it. Seeing her dart into the living room, the squirrel ran around her, back out where it came from. The sliding glass doors that led to the backyard stood wide open. The heavy humidity of the outdoors seeped into the air-conditioned space.

"Strange," she said to herself before walking over to close the door. She made sure to lock it and then tugged at it to make sure it was secure.

She returned to the kitchen to pour herself a cup of coffee, hoping the caffeine would help with her headache. Leaning against the counter, she looked out to the living room, holding the warm cup in her hand. She had been thinking about painting the walls a pale yellow when a tiny brown and white bird flew in and landed on the bar in front of her. It looked at her with small black eyes.

"Where did you come from?" She walked up to the bird who tweeted and cocked its head at her. It took off in flight, pumping its wings a few times before gliding out the sliding glass door that she had just locked.

"Impossible." A pit opened up in her stomach. She set her coffee on the bar and went over. She pulled the door closed and locked it again. This time she tested it three times to make sure it was really secure.

**

Stephanie and Will bought a patio furniture set from the

local big box store. It was perfect for their paved patio in the backyard. Stephanie imagined them having friends over to sit outside in the cool winter months. The yard would make a perfect place for entertaining. As they sat in the dusty light of the evening assembling the patio furniture, the sounds from the wilderness just beyond the fence rose in the air. The chorus of croaks, squeaks, and screeches continued to make Stephanie feel unsafe even though she'd hoped to eventually find them relaxing. She sat holding the screwdriver and staring at the fence.

"What's wrong?" Will asked. He had just finished assembling the loveseat.

Stephanie shook her head. "Nothing." Just then, a deep growl rumbled through the air, and something knocked against the other side of the fence. Stephanie jumped back, dropping her screwdriver. "What was that?"

"The monster is coming to get you." Will chuckled.

"Not funny." She put her hands on her hips.

"It was nothing. Probably a raccoon." He picked up the screwdriver she'd dropped.

Stephanie knew he was probably right. They weren't in the middle of the wilderness. The nature preserve on the other side of their fence sat in the middle of a residential, suburban neighborhood. There probably weren't any panthers or bobcats there. They were nothing to stress out about. The animals she heard were animals that you could hear in just about every Florida neighborhood, but for some reason, in this backyard, everything seemed a bit more intense, including her fear. Feeling a bit nauseous, she stood up. "I have to go inside. The mosquitoes are getting to me."

"I see how it is." Will could sit outside for hours and never get bitten. Stephanie wasn't that lucky. Even though the bugs weren't biting tonight, she could use it as an excuse to go inside.

Relief washed over her when she stepped back into the house. It was her sanctuary from the outside world. That was exactly what she had meant it to be. She sighed, sat down on the stiff leather sofa, and closed her eyes for a moment. In the silence, she swore she heard something up the hall. A scratching sound came from the back bedroom. She stood up and looked out the glass doors where Will was finishing up putting together the chair that she had given up on. She considered going out and getting him to investigate the sound but thought better of it. She was a grown woman who could deal with these things on her own. She went to the kitchen pantry and pulled out a broom before creeping silently down the hallway. She listened at the closed door. Something fell to the floor with a crash followed by the sound of scurrying across the tile.

She took a deep breath, turned the doorknob, and pushed the door open, making sure to flick on the light as she did. An opossum scurried away from her, disappearing into the closet at the back corner of the room. Stephanie stood in the doorway, holding the broom like a weapon, and considering her options. Part of her wanted to pull the door closed and get Will to take care of it, but another part of her wanted to be a grown-up and deal with the opossum herself. The part of her that wanted to be a grown-up won. She tiptoed into the room, holding the broom out in front of her. She watched the door, expecting to see the opossum come running out at any moment. She used the broom to push the door open, revealing a dark closet that seemed bigger than she remembered. A chain hung from an exposed compact fluorescent lightbulb in the ceiling. The chain swung back and forth, drawing her attention upward. She searched every inch of the closet with her eyes. No opossum. She'd seen it run inside. It had to be there. She pulled the chain, baptizing the closet in harsh white light. Still no opossum.

Stephanie walked into the closet and stood in the center of the floor, puzzling over where the opossum went when she heard a noise in the wall. Something scratched at the plaster like an animal trying to dig its way out of the wall. Stephanie screeched and dropped the broom.

Will came running up the hall. "What happened? What is it?"

She pointed at the back wall of the closet. "Listen. There's something in there."

Will squeezed past her, placing his ear against the wall.

She stood perfectly still, watching him, imagining whatever it was breaking through the wall and biting his ear off.

After only a few moments of listening, he took his ear away. "I'll call an exterminator tomorrow," he said.

She wished that was the only animal she'd seen in the house, but it wasn't. She swore she saw raccoons, mice, frogs, and all manner of creatures. They'd wander up the hallway like they belonged in the house. They meandered through the living room while she was watching television. They waited for her in the bathroom in the middle of the night. Only she saw them. The animals never hung around for Will. She called exterminators and wildlife catchers who poked around their home, looking for cracks, gaps, and places where animals could get in to nest. They never found anything. The roofing was all intact, and there were no holes in the stucco. The house had been sealed up completely and should have been pest free, but it wasn't.

The animals in the house weren't the only problem. If they were, Stephanie would've been able to manage somehow. As the days progressed, so did their problems. There weren't just wild animals trying to get in. Something much more sinister wanted in too.

Chapter 3

"How are the animals getting in?" Cheryl asked.

"Nobody knows." Stephanie stood and went to the kitchen. "I need a drink. Does anyone want anything?"

They all shook their heads. She got a beer out of the refrigerator. "Do you want a second one?" she asked Will.

"No. I'm good." He held up the beer he was already drinking.

Cheryl kept thinking about the animals. How did they get into the house? What could it possibly mean? So far, this seemed like a problem for an exterminator, not for paranormal investigators. There must've been something she was missing.

"What happened next?" Adam asked.

"I don't quite understand why you ended up calling Day about this," Cheryl said.

"Should I tell them, or do you want to?" Will set his bottle on the floor next to him.

They all looked into the kitchen where Stephanie stood with the refrigerator door still open behind her, looking at the living room wall just above Cheryl and Adam's heads. Her mouth hung slack. Her eyes were open wide.

"Stephanie!" Cheryl knew something was wrong as soon as she saw the twisted expression of fear on her face. Cheryl turned and looked behind her, hoping to see something, but she only saw a blank white wall.

Everyone got to their feet. Will reached Stephanie first. "Steph, what's wrong?" He stood in front of her holding her shoulders. He gave her a little shake to snap her out of her trance, but she didn't move. She stayed perfectly still, her eyes transfixed on the wall.

Cheryl looked back at Stephanie and noticed swarms of bugs pouring into the kitchen from every crack in the wall. They came from the cabinets and drawers. They scuttled out from under the stove. Hundreds of roaches, worms, millipedes, and beetles all gathered in the center of the kitchen floor. They crawled across each other, piling on top of one another to form the shape of a woman. Her body was a constant wave of motion as the insects crawled over each other. The woman's form wasn't concrete. She seemed to flicker in and out of existence, like a television channel when the reception is bad.

No one else in the room reacted to this disturbing sight. Cheryl knew that this woman had to be the one responsible for all of this. The woman stretched once her body had completely formed. She reached her arms high over her head and opened her mouth in a yawn. Then she bent down to the ground, and a fat opossum appeared out of nowhere and crawled up her arm, settling on her shoulders.

"What are you doing here? What do you want?" Cheryl walked quickly into the kitchen around the woman so she could get a good look at her. She got a glimpse of her face before she flickered away, vanishing. On her narrow face were deep black holes where the eyes should've been. She blinked away as abruptly as she'd appeared.

"Did you see that?" Cheryl looked over at Adam, who stood staring at the wall in the living room with an astonished look on his face. Surely, he saw something there that Cheryl didn't.

**

Adam rushed over to Stephanie. He knew how traumatic seeing something that challenged your sense of reality could be, and Stephanie was obviously having that experience.

When he approached her, he recognized the look on her face. He'd had that look on his own face in the past. He followed her gaze to the living room wall just above the sofa. A hole had opened up there that looked like a window into another world. In this other world, it was night. Tiny yellow stars dotted the midnight blue sky. Some of them streaked across the night, leaving trails of light behind them. Bobcats skulked amongst the tall trees. Coyotes loped along in the grass. It would have been a beautiful scene if it wasn't for the dread it brought. Adam couldn't quite describe it, but something about it wrapped him in fear. His breathing increased, and he took a step toward the hole. He noticed Cheryl looking at him.

"Can you see what I'm seeing?" He pointed at the wall.

Cheryl looked at it and then back at him. She shook her head. "No. What are you seeing?"

Adam was about to describe the scene when the opening started filling up with a thick black liquid. A high-pitched ring sliced through him. It shot into his ears so loudly that he couldn't hear anything else. The noise increased in volume as the black viscous fluid undulated and rose over the hole, obscuring Adam's view. Once the scene was completely gone, the hole sealed up. Adam rushed over to it and put his hand where it had been. The smooth white plaster left no trace of what had just happened.

He was lost in his own world of disbelief for a few

moments before he turned around to see Stephanie moving again. She pointed directly at him.

"Did you see that?" Her voice quivered. "A hole opened up in the wall that looked right into the woods." Stephanie was breathless as she described the same scene Adam had just seen, but there was one difference. "And there was a woman too. She was right here in front of me."

Adam hadn't seen a woman but didn't doubt Stephanie had seen something he hadn't.

"What did she look like?" Cheryl asked.

Stephanie swallowed, and her expression went blank. "I don't remember."

"That's okay," Cheryl said. "Maybe it's best that you don't."

"Why?" Stephanie drew her eyebrows together. "Did you see her too?"

Cheryl nodded.

"That means I'm not crazy." She raised her eyebrows, and her forehead creased.

"She was standing right there." Cheryl pointed to the spot on the floor just in front of Stephanie.

"I wanted to run away, but I couldn't." A tear rolled down Stephanie's cheek, and she wiped it away.

Adam shook off the shock he was feeling. "I didn't see the woman, but I saw the hole. It was right there."

"That's right." Stephanie's voice rose with excitement. She turned her attention to Will. "See, they saw it too."

Her pleading tone made Adam wonder what their conversations were like when no one else was around.

"I didn't see anything," Will said, shaking his head.

"Most people can't," Adam said. "It's surprising that Stephanie can."

"You can fix this, right?" Stephanie's hopeful gaze fell on Cheryl. "I know you can."

"Yes." Adam wanted to make everything right so badly that he didn't wait for Cheryl's answer. If he felt like it could be fixed, he would fix it. They never started a case with an obvious solution. That was fine. That's what they were used to. Adam wouldn't let not knowing how stop him from trying. "But you have to tell us everything. Even if you're not sure if something is worth mentioning, mention it."

Stephanie looked at Day. "I'm willing to tell you everything. Just ask Day."

"She'll tell you everything she can think of and more." Day smiled.

Adam set up a few night vision motion-activated cameras in the house while Stephanie, Cheryl, and Day talked in hushed tones. Will hovered over him, watching his every move.

"So, do you ever really pick anything up on these?" He picked up one of the small rectangular cameras to examine.

Adam looked at him and grimaced. "Sometimes. It depends on what's going on with the case." He reached out his hand, motioning for Will to hand him the camera.

"Sorry," Will muttered before handing it over to him. "I was just curious."

Adam pursed his lips and shook his head. He needed to relax, but it was so hard after all he'd seen. "No. I'm sorry, man."

"I shouldn't have messed with your camera without asking. It was presumptuous." Will shoved his hands into his pockets and rocked forward on the balls of his feet.

"Our last case was a lot to deal with, and I'm still on edge." Adam put the camera in his hand on a tripod.

"Stephanie told me. It sounded intense. A serial killer--I can't even imagine." He paused and leaned in closer to Adam.

"You didn't really see anything before, did you?" He narrowed his eyes at Adam.

Adam nodded wearily. "Yes, I did. I saw it as clear as I can see you now."

Will cocked his head and looked at Adam with skepticism. "Okay." He nodded a few times. "I was going to ask how you deal with all of this, but--" He gestured at Adam with his open hand. "You obviously believe in this stuff."

Adam chuckled. "I wouldn't be doing this if I didn't." He picked up the open black duffle bag on the floor, and the contents clattered against each other. He turned to walk up the hallway to the living room where the women sat on the sofa talking, but Will caught hold of his arm.

"I agreed to this because I thought it would make Stephanie feel better. I think she's just stressed from the move and starting her new job." He paused and clamped his mouth closed for a few seconds before continuing. "Do me a favor and leave the camera set up for a few days and then just tell her that whatever she thinks is going on here is gone. Maybe then we'll be able to get back to normal."

This wasn't the first time Adam had gotten a request like this. "I can't do that."

Will scowled. "Come on. Don't you want her to stop worrying?"

Stephanie was like family to Cheryl. That made her like family to Adam too. "Of course, I do. That's why I'm going to do my best to get to the bottom of whatever is going on here."

"Don't you think that if there really was something going on, I would've experienced it too?" He let go of Adam's arm.

"Not necessarily. People assume certain places are haunted when in reality a lot of the time it's not a place at all, it's the person who's haunted." Adam had explained this more times than he could count now.

"But why her?" Will drew his eyebrows together.

"That's what we have to figure out." Adam started toward the living room again.

Will stood at the end of the hallway, looking defeated. "Don't think I'm rude, but I have some things I need to get done." He pointed at the bedroom door.

"Go ahead. Once I'm finished setting up, we'll get going." Normally Adam would be open to answering questions, but the last week had been so full on that he only wanted some quiet time.

"If you could let them know--" He pointed down the hallway.

"No, problem."

He went into the bedroom and closed the door behind him.

Once all the cameras were ready to go, Adam went back into the living room to see the three women sitting on the sofa.

"Where's Will?" Stephanie asked.

"He said he had some things he needed to take care of." Adam put his duffle bag down on the floor next to his feet.

The puzzled look on Stephanie's face told him that she thought this was strange. She crossed her arms and sat back on the sofa. "He doesn't believe me."

"He will eventually. These things can be hard to believe." Day rubbed her shoulder.

"All set?" Cheryl asked.

"Hopefully, we'll catch something that will help us unravel this mystery," he said to Stephanie.

"Even if we don't catch anything on camera, we will unravel this mystery," Cheryl reassured her. "We always do. I'm going to do some research about the property when I get home to see if I can find anything interesting. If we can clear whatever terrible thing happened here in the past, all of this negative energy will go away, and you two can live happily ever after." Cheryl added a comforting smile to the end of her sentence.

**

They'd barely gotten out of Stephanie's neighborhood when Cheryl's phone rang. She fished it out of the bottom of her purse, where it lay nestled beneath a deck of tarot cards and a few stray crystals. "It's Day," she said before answering.

"Hey," she said into the phone. "What did you think about what happened today?"

Day cleared her throat. "It's happened before, and I think it's worrying."

"Yes, it is. The fact that she's actually seen something is weird. I've only seen that a couple of times." Most hauntings were based more on feelings and dreams. That was most of Cheryl's experience with her clients unless they had special abilities similar to her own.

"I can feel it when I walk into the house," Day said. "Whatever it is feels ancient."

"What's she saying?" Adam asked as they merged onto the highway.

Cheryl took the phone away from her ear. "I'll put her on speaker." She held the phone out in front of her. "You're on speakerphone." She spoke unnecessarily loudly.

Day continued, her voice tinny now. "This energy has been in the house for a long time. I've only been helping them with it for about a week. So far, I've tried burning sage and making a spiritual barrier around the house, but it hasn't seemed to work. Whatever it is has attached to the land the house is on. You felt what was going on in the backyard."

"We both did," Adam said.

"Everyone seems to feel it in the backyard, except Will. I don't know how that's possible, but from what he tells me, he doesn't feel anything. "

Everything Day said was stuff they had already discussed at the house, but Cheryl enjoyed going over it again with her. "Nothing you did made a difference at all?"

"No. Not yet." Day was always hopeful.

Cheryl hadn't talked to Stephanie as much as she once did. She was so busy with her new business, and Stephanie was busy with her new fiancé. It seemed like they had less time to catch up. Cheryl regretted that. Stephanie was the first friend she made when she was still new in town. Back then, she was so paranoid about Mark finding her that she hardly had the brain space to think about much else. Stephanie had been like a life raft for her.

"I can't believe everything you told me about Mark." Day seemed to be picking up on her thoughts.

Cheryl smiled. The idea of Mark being out there free to harm other people had haunted her even before she'd known the true horror of what he had done. Knowing he was gone once and for all gave her more relief than she could even begin to explain. "I'm just glad it's all over."

"So am I," Adam chimed in.

"It's great to finally have him out of my life." That was something Cheryl never thought would happen, not even the day she left. "Anyway, I'll do some research when I get home. We're going to figure out what's going on at Stephanie and Will's. I hope you'll keep doing the investigation with us."

"I'm not getting in the way?" Day asked.

"Are you kidding me? Of course not." Cheryl chuckled at the thought. Day had been a mentor to her. She was honored to work with her on a case, and she had no idea how quickly this case would escalate. They would need all the help they could get.

Chapter 4

Adam was glad to be home. He hadn't had one minute to relax since they'd finished their case in Ridge Point. His bedroom was a mess, but he wasn't going to worry about it. He needed a moment to sit down in silence and think about everything that had happened. During the past few months, his world had practically turned on its head. He laid across his bed and closed his eyes to take a quick nap.

He had just drifted off when he noticed the twittering of birds around him. When he opened his eyes, he was no longer lying across his bed. He was on the ground beneath a large oak tree. Its branches twisted to the sky. Roots like tentacles wrapped around the flat gray boulder it grew on before finding their way into the earth. Adam sat up. Disoriented, he looked around him only to come face to face with a coyote. It sat on its haunches, staring at him with one amber eye in the middle of its forehead. Adam blinked, thinking that this was all a dream, then remembering what he had read in the book the bookkeeper had given him. "New visionaries can see parallel worlds." Was this what he was seeing now?

A sense of calm settled over him. The dew on the grass soaked through his pants. Tiny pebbles in the dirt dug into his palms. The coyote opened its mouth to howl, but a high-pitched scream came out instead. The noise, long and loud, sliced through the night air. When it stopped howling, it returned its gaze to Adam. Its coarse sandy fur gleamed in the moonlight. Its tongue lolled from its mouth as it panted, showing pointed, yellowing teeth. Losing interest in him, the coyote turned and trotted off. Adam felt the desire to follow it. He stood and took one step, and then another, and on his third step, found himself back in his bedroom. It was dark outside now. His blinds were open. The lights from the streetlamps cast a blue glow on his bedroom wall. When he went to turn on the light switch, he noticed something gritty beneath his feet. Flipping the switch to illuminate his room revealed a small mound of black dirt at the foot of his bed.

**

Cheryl had only been out of town for a few days, but her mailbox was jammed with mail, mostly overdue bills. She had a drawer full of threats from collection agencies. Everyone wanted money from her, but she had no money to give. She stood in front of the trash can by the mailboxes, dropping the pink envelopes in. She didn't want to look at them anymore. She didn't have time to worry about finances. It seemed like she was in a never-ending hole.

As she went up the stairs to her apartment, the man behind her didn't realize that she knew that he was following her. His black turtleneck and jeans were inappropriate for the hot weather. It was unusually hot for winter. Usually, the Bay area had a bit of relief in the winter months. Sometimes the temperature could even drop into the forties, but not this year. The heat was unrelenting. Still, this man chose to wear a turtleneck and black leather jacket. He was most definitely dead. She suspected as much because she didn't hear the echo of his footsteps on the stairs. Instead of wondering what he wanted and letting him continue to stalk her, she turned around on the landing.

"You know I can see you, don't you?"

Taken aback, the man stopped. He froze as if staying still would make him invisible to her.

"What do you want?"

He pointed at his chest and then looked behind him before looking back at her. "Are you talking to me?"

"Who else would I be talking to? You're the only one here."

He smiled, revealing two rows of perfect white teeth. "You're right. I am the only one here, aren't I?" He chuckled. "Imagine that. I'm here, and you're talking to me. Little old me."

There was nothing little about him. He towered over Cheryl by at least a foot, and his muscular shoulders bulged beneath his jacket. "What do you need?"

"What do you mean?" he wrinkled his forehead at her.

"You must be following me for a reason. Usually, you would have some unfinished business that you want me to help you take care of." She put her hands on her hips and let out an exasperated breath.

He cleared his throat and looked at the floor. "You might think this is a strange thing to ask."

Cheryl wondered what favor he might request. She was getting to the point where she felt like she had heard just about everything a ghost would possibly want to tell her.

"But..." He reached his hand into his pocket, and Cheryl heard a squelching sound that unsettled her stomach. She looked down to see a dark stain around the pocket of his pants spreading down his leg. He pulled something red in squishy from his pocket, and when he held it out in his hand, it grew in size like an inflating balloon. A beating heart lay in his hand, gently thumping. "I need to return this to the owner."

Cheryl gasped and held her hand over her mouth in shock.

He threw his head back in an opened mouth laugh. Then he raised his hand next to his head and lobbed the heart in Cheryl's direction. Cheryl ducked and let out a yelp. She froze, crouched down on the stairs waiting to feel the warm wet organ strike her. Nothing happened. Her neighbor, Mr. Duncan, came down the stairs led by his white terrier.

"Are you okay?" he asked. The dog jumped up, scratching her bare leg with its blunt claws. Mr. Duncan gave the leash a yank.

Cheryl straightened up. "Yes, I'm fine." She hiked her purse up on her shoulder. "How have you been?" She bent over to pet the scruffy white terrier who panted excitedly. "And how are you Miss Daisy?" She raised her voice an octave. The dog jumped up on her again.

"I haven't seen you around." Mr. Duncan looked over her shoulder as he spoke to her like he was in a hurry to leave.

"Yeah. I went to my hometown for a little bit."

He nodded. "That's interesting. You've been having a lot of parties recently."

"What do you mean? I only got home this morning." Mr. Duncan was quiet enough, but he was often suspicious. He was always looking for a reason to report her to management.

"You certainly were making a lot of noise for someone who wasn't home." He grimaced.

Cheryl stared at him blankly. "I swear, I've been gone since Friday. You must've heard somebody else. Maybe the guys that live above you. They used to have some pretty loud parties."

Mr. Duncan shook his head as he walked down the stairs. "It was definitely coming from your apartment. Don't do it again. You need to have more consideration for your neighbors." His dog still stood on the step in front of Cheryl. He yanked the leash, and she clambered down the stairs, her nails clicking on the concrete.

He was wrong, and she knew it. She didn't need to prove herself. She let him go, and she continued up to her apartment, hoping not to see that ghost with the heart again.

She wanted to make sure she did some research about Stephanie's house before her shift on the Psychic Hotline started. A few searches and her investigation turned up absolutely nothing. This would be harder than she'd anticipated. There wasn't much beyond the history of the nature reserve. She was reading a long, drawn-out article about why the land was never developed with Beau, her faithful tabby, curled in her lap when she heard a crash in the kitchen. She jumped out of her skin, waking the snoozing cat, who looked up at her with his yellow-green eyes before skulking off to the opposite corner of the sofa. "What was that?"

She tiptoed into the kitchen, expecting to see another ghost there, but her tiny galley kitchen was empty. Nothing was out of place. No one living or dead was there. Maybe she'd heard the neighbors upstairs. That's what she convinced herself of before returning to her seat. When she picked up her laptop again and placed it in her lap, she noticed the article she was reading was no longer on the screen. A black and white photo of a tree growing on a large flat boulder filled her screen. The roots, like the tentacles of an octopus, hugged the large stone into the bottom of the trunk. She'd never seen a tree growing like that before, and if she wasn't wondering how the picture got on her screen in the first place, she might've wondered how a tree came to be growing on a rock like that. Cheryl leaned into the screen to get a closer look at the image. She hit the scroll down button, but as soon as she touched the keyboard, the screen flashed, returning to the article she had previously been reading. "What was that?" she asked Beau, who blinked up at her before returning his head to the cushion and closing his eyes. She hit the back button on the website, and it just took her back to her original search. "I don't understand?"

When Cheryl closed her eyes to sleep that night, she saw the tree in her mind. The image was so clear that it was like she was looking at the photo again. She tried to think of reasons for its appearance on her computer as she drifted off.

Cheryl awoke to the rhythmic thud of a bass drum and a wave of conversation. Someone somewhere screeched before the crowd broke into laughter. It was a party, and the sound was so loud that it seemed to be happening in her apartment. She rolled out of bed and angrily stomped into her living room. The music rose, and the room seemed to shake.

This must've been what Mr. Duncan was talking about. She picked up her phone to check the time. It was two in the morning. The noise swelled. This was unacceptable. Even though she did her best not to be one of those neighbors, she pulled on a pair of shorts. She'd have to go upstairs to ask them to keep it down. She'd never done anything like that before, but she'd never heard a party this loud before either. She was trying to decide what to do when someone knocked on her door.

Whack, whack, whack. Who would be knocking at this hour? Fear coursed through her.

Whack, whack, whack. Again.

She wanted to run to her bedroom and hide beneath the covers.

"Police... open up!"

Cheryl scowled at her door. Why were the police at her

place?

She hurried to the door and looked through the keyhole. What appeared to be to officers dressed in their black uniforms stood there with their arms crossed. This couldn't be right. Cautiously, she opened the door a crack. The officers narrowed their eyes as they tried to look past her into her dark apartment.

"What's this about?" she asked. All of the music and noise stopped. Cheryl pictured the people in the apartment above her falling silent when the police knocked on their door too. She thought it would be funny if they all froze like statues.

"We got a call about a party."

"That's not going on here. It must be upstairs. It woke me up too." She was sure Mr. Duncan had called the police, unconvinced that she wasn't the one doing all the partying.

"Do you mind if we come in and take a look?" one of the officers asked.

Cheryl did mind, but she was afraid to say no. In situations like this, she always felt like there was never a right answer. The police could come in, and even though there was no reason for a problem to arise, they could find one. Or she could tell them they couldn't come in, and they could force their way in and find a problem that way. Either way was risky. This time she decided to cooperate.

She swung the door open wide and stepped to the side. "Come on in and see." She reached over slowly and turned on the lamp. She didn't want them to think she was reaching for a weapon.

They took wide, confident strides as they walked around her apartment. They walked in a circle around her living room then went into her kitchen. Then they doubled back and looked into her bedroom. One of them even wandered into the bathroom, and she wondered if they thought she was hiding a party in there.

"There doesn't seem to be anyone here," one of the officers said.

Cheryl tried to keep her face as still as possible because she didn't want anything to be interpreted as her lying to them. "Like I said, there's nobody here. I wasn't the one having a party."

"You weren't making any noise at all?" the officer asked, looking at her with a puzzled expression.

Cheryl shook her head. "I think it was coming from upstairs. I guess it doesn't matter now since it stopped."

They were all silent for a moment.

"Sounds like it did." The other officer walked to the door. "Sorry for the inconvenience."

"Have a good night." They left.

She was happy to have her apartment to herself again. Now that it was quiet, maybe she could get some sleep. Stephanie and Will's haunting case was only just beginning. She needed to get rest so she could be fresh enough to think about how to help them, if she even could.

Chapter 5

"Steph, what are you doing out here?"

Stephanie felt Will's arm wrap around her shoulder. She opened her eyes to find herself standing in the backyard in her nightgown. Dew covered her feet. Stray blades of grass stuck to her ankles. The porch light sent a harsh white halo of light into the night.

"Are you okay?" Will narrowed his eyes at her before squinting at the darkness. "Is there something out here?"

She shook her head and tried to orient herself. "I don't know what happened. I must have been sleepwalking." She had never sleepwalked before. The last thing she remembered was climbing into bed that night. She'd rolled over onto her side and closed her eyes, anxious to get some rest. Sleeping had been difficult for her ever since moving into the house, but now that Adam, Cheryl, and Day were all on the case, she felt a bit more optimistic. Thinking about that was the last thing she remembered before drifting off to sleep.

"I kept calling your name, but you wouldn't answer or even turn around." Will let go of her shoulder.

Stephanie looked up. A dusting of stars covered the dark sky.

"Let's go back to bed." Will turned around and walked toward the patio.

Lovelyn Bettison

"Okay." Turning on her heels, she ran after him.

In the bathroom, she used a towel to dry her feet and knock off the stray bits of grass. Will had already gone back to bed. He was able to fall asleep so quickly.

As she rubbed her foot with the towel, she thought she heard something, a scraping sound inside the sink vanity.

"Oh no," she said to herself. Dropping the towel on the floor, she walked over and squatted in front of the sink. Something was scurrying around inside. She could imagine it knocking down the bottle of hydrogen peroxide and tearing the extra rolls of toilet paper to shreds. The cabinet door clattered. Stephanie reached for the handle with a slow, shaking hand. Whatever was inside squeaked, and she jumped back. She went into the dark bedroom to get Will. He was snoring heavily now. She shook his shoulder. "Wake up!" She looked back at the bathroom door, expecting to see a creature scuttle across the floor at her, but there was nothing. Will rolled over and groaned.

If he got up, what would he do anyway? He would open the cabinet door, and whatever was inside would come running out. She didn't want that, not tonight. Stephanie went to the kitchen and found a metal shish kebab stick. Then tiptoeing back into the bathroom, she slipped the stick through the handles on the vanity to secure it. She shut off the bathroom light, closed the door, and shoved the towel beneath it just in case anything got out in the bathroom. Then she went back to bed. Somehow she managed to drift off to sleep.

"What do you mean... there's something in the bathroom cabinet?" Will asked the next morning.

"Didn't you notice that I locked it closed with a shish

kebab stick?" He had gotten up before Stephanie. She was still exhausted from the night before.

"I was wondering what that was about." Wrapped in a towel, he stood in the doorway to the walk-in closet.

"Did you open it?" She had hoped he'd take care of whatever was inside without her having to be involved.

"Nope." He started looking through his clothes.

"Will you?"

He peeked his head out of the closet to look at her. "Do you want me to?"

"I don't want to." Stephanie looked at the bathroom door that was now open. His shower had left a foggy haze over the mirror.

He let out a sigh and went into the bathroom. Stephanie followed him on tiptoes. He slid the stick out from the handles of the vanity cabinet and opened the doors. There was nothing living beneath the sink, but there'd obviously been something. Just as Stephanie had imagined, bottles were overturned, and two rolls of toilet paper were shredded. The pieces were piled up on the bottom of the cabinet, like a white nest.

"Rats," Will said. He pulled out the strands of toilet paper, some of them sticking to his still-damp hands. They cascaded onto the floor. "How did they get in?" He pulled a box of Band-Aids, extra bottles of shampoo, a bag of cotton balls. Once he got to the back, he looked around.

"What do you see?" she asked.

"I don't understand how anything could have gotten in here. It's all sealed up around the pipes. There are no other holes." He didn't look for long. He got up and looked at his hands with annoyance, seeing the flecks of toilet paper stuck to them. He wiped them on his towel. "I have to get ready for work. We can take care this later."

"Okay," Stephanie said. He squeezed past her as she stood in the bathroom doorway, looking at the mess beneath the vanity.

Will hurried through the house, getting dressed and fixing coffee. She could hear his heavy footsteps. She smelled the rich aroma of the coffee brewing, but she stood frozen, looking at the mound of shredded paper and the overturned bottles in the vanity. Both doors gaped open. What had been inside? Where had it gone?

Will hurried into the bedroom. "Steph!" She didn't even turn around when she heard him. He hurried up behind her. Putting his arms around her waist, he kissed her neck. "What are you doing still standing here? You've got to get dressed and go to work."

She looked down at her rumpled nightgown. He was right. She wouldn't have much time to get ready. She shook off the trance she'd fallen into and rushed over to the closet. "I'm going to be late."

"Don't drive like a maniac to get to work on time," Will said as he rushed out of the bedroom.

Stephanie was still in a daze when she got to work. She hardly remembered driving there. She kept thinking about the vanity. Something was definitely in there. Every time she would think about it, or how she had ended up in the backyard sleepwalking, she felt sick. Bile rose from her stomach, burning the back of her throat. She swallowed it down and hoped she wouldn't get sick at work. She parked in her office parking lot and checked her reflection in the rearview mirror before getting out of the car. She walked quickly across the blacktop. She was a few minutes late but hoped no one would notice. As she stepped inside, she kept her head down and made her way to her office. Normally, she made a big point of arriving at work, saying hello to everyone, and smiling brightly. She was still new in the office and trying her best to make a good impression, but not today. Today she hoped no one noticed her arrival, and they didn't. She had managed to sneak in quietly. No one even lifted their head to glance at her as she walked down the hall.

She flipped on the overhead fluorescent light in her windowless office. She stuck her purse in the drawer on the top left. Then she pulled out her chair. She looked down before sitting, and her heart began to race. Sitting in the chair was the stuffed bear the girl had left at her house with its patchy fur, embroidered heart, and missing button eye. It was just a stuffed bear, but it looked so sinister sitting there. She put her hand up to her mouth and gasped.

Just then, her coworker Anne peeked her head inside her office. "Everything okay in here?"

Stephanie shook her head. She pointed at the bear. "Did someone put this in my office?"

Anne followed the line of her finger to the chair, where the stuffed bear sat happily. "Not that I know of. Nicole came in with her son for a little bit yesterday after you left. Maybe it's his?"

She knew it wasn't his. She knew from the embroidered heart and the worn patches of fur. She had examined that bear over and over again since finding it on her bed. After showing it to Cheryl, she'd tucked it away in the coat closet in the living room out of sight.

Anne glanced over at her again and then laughed. "Don't look so scared. It's just a stuffed bear."

Stephanie went over and picked it up roughly, holding it by the neck. "You're right. I don't know why, but it freaked me out."

"Give it to me." Anne reached out her hand. "I'll take it to Nicole."

"Thanks." Stephanie was happy to get rid of it.

For the rest of the day, she couldn't think straight. Her thoughts kept drifting off. At one point, she even fell asleep on her desk. Luckily, no one seemed to notice.

At six o'clock, she gathered up her things, put her purse over her shoulder, and started out of the office. When she passed Anne's door, Anne called out to her. "Stephanie, the bear wasn't Ryan's."

Stephanie stopped. "Who?"

"Ryan, Nicole's son." Anne got up. She picked up the bear that had been sitting on the corner of her desk and walked over to Stephanie with it. She handed it to her. "It looks like you have a new toy." She snickered.

Stephanie rolled her eyes. "Keep it. What am I going to do with it?"

Anne looked down at the stuffed animal in her hand. "I guess I can throw it away. If it were in better shape, I'd donate it or give it to someone's kid as a gift."

"Throw it away, then." When Stephanie walked out of the office, she hoped she'd never see the bear again, but somewhere inside, she knew she would.

**

Day was helping a customer, so Adam hung around the entrance of the store, perusing the bookshelves. He liked Day, but always felt uncomfortable hanging out in her store. It wasn't his type of place, too many crystals and New Age books. Even though he was a partner in Suncoast Paranormal, he was still getting used to the idea of being part of this world. His analytical mind had difficulty believing sometimes. Looking at the books about chakras and healing energy made him feel a bit strange. Was he associated with this type of thing now? It all seemed made up to him, and now he was the one having visions and seeing ghosts. There was a constant push-pull that made him unsure of how to characterize himself. Yet here he was with a tiny piece of quartz in one pocket and a small vial of holy water in the other.

"You'll be fine," Day said to her customer. "Just do what I told you."

"Thank you so much." The customer, a young woman with a headful of messy, purple hair and a nose ring, took the bag from the counter. "I hope you're right." She hurried to the door and smiled at Adam as she pushed it open.

Adam smiled back.

"No Cheryl?" Day walked over to him and kissed him on both cheeks like they were in a French movie.

"She said she would meet us here." Adam had talked to her first thing that morning, and she seemed tired and anxious but hadn't said why.

"That's strange. You two usually travel together these days." She grinned in the way that people do when they're keeping a secret. He wondered what she knew that he didn't.

"Can I ask you something?" He ran his hand along the edge of the bookshelf next to him.

Her grin widened. "You just did."

Adam should've expected that. His sister used to do the same thing. "Something else."

"Of course. You can ask me anything." Her expression grew serious as she took a step toward him.

"Okay."

Day had been Cheryl's mentor, and Adam wondered if she

could be the same for him. All of these dreams and visions made him feel like he was in a bit over his head much of the time. He hadn't talked to anyone about it besides Cheryl. Maybe Day could help him interpret the things he saw. "Have you ever heard of something called *A Book For New Visionaries?*"

Day scanned the bookshelves quickly as if looking for the title among her inventory. "I don't think so. Who is the author?"

Adam thought for a moment. "I don't know." He hadn't recalled seeing an author's name anywhere on the book. He looked at the book so many times now that he would have remembered it if it were there.

"I'm pretty sure I don't have it in the store, but I could order it for you if you want. What's it about?" she asked as she walked over to the counter and pulled out a tablet.

"I already have it."

She looked up from the screen at him. "Oh, I thought you wanted me to get it for you." She tapped the screen a few times and then stuck the tablet back under the counter. "What's your question then?"

He took a deep breath. "Have you ever heard of a visionary?"

"Do you mean someone who sees visions?" she asked.

"Kind of but it's more specific than that. Someone who can see a world parallel to our own." No matter how many times he read about it or experienced it himself, he still wasn't exactly sure what a visionary was.

She leaned forward, resting her elbows on the counter and her chin on her hands. "I haven't, but I want to hear more."

He dropped his shoulders. He was hoping she'd be able to explain some of this to him, not the other way around. "I get these visions of things that are happening. They're not dreams because when they're over, I have physical evidence from them like my pants will be wet, or I have dirt on the bottom of my feet."

"I've read books about things like this happening to people before."

He wasn't the only one, even though he felt like he was. "It hasn't been happening long, only about a month, if that. I'm officially a weirdo now." He laughed dryly.

"There's nothing wrong with being a little strange, is there?" She walked around the counter to a bookshelf near the door and ran her index finger along the spines of a row of books.

"It depends on what kind of strange." Adam had been wondering if his new ability was more of a curse than a blessing.

She pulled a book from the shelf. "Here. This one explains a bit about what you're talking about," she said as she held it out to him.

Adam walked over and took the book from her, but he didn't bother looking at it. He wasn't interested in another book. He wanted to talk to someone in real life. "I don't know why this stuff is happening to me. I'm trying to use it to help out with our investigations, but sometimes I get these visions, and I don't know what they're supposed to help with." There was desperation in his voice. "I just don't know what to do."

Day creased her forehead. "I'm sorry. Sounds like it's been really terrible for you."

"It's not that. I just need some advice."

"What kind of advice are you looking for?" She glanced down at the book in his hand.

Remembering he was holding it, he flipped through the pages, a gesture of respect more than curiosity about the contents. When he thought he had looked at it enough, he continued. "I'm not sure how to handle all of this. What's going on with Cheryl and me--" What was he asking? Did he even know? "It's been a lot."

"I'm sure it has been. You just came back from a really intense case, and now you're on another. Plus you're still working at your other job, right?"

He hadn't been there in ages, but he was still on call. "Yeah."

She reached out and took hold of his forearm. "Anyone would feel pressure in this situation. That's natural. As far as what to do with this new ability you've found yourself with, I don't know what to tell you other than to relax and go with it. You're seeing these things for a reason." She let go of his arm and let her hand fall to her side. "Have they helped you with any cases?"

Adam nodded. Since he'd started having them, they'd helped with every case. "Yes."

"Well then, that's the most important thing, isn't it? It looks like you and Cheryl have more in common than I initially thought." She smiled softly.

"Yeah."

Day glanced down at the narrow watch she wore on her thin wrist. "Speaking of Cheryl, where is she? She's late."

Adam pulled his phone from his pocket and looked at the clock. She was right. Cheryl was fifteen minutes late. Even though she seemed a bit scatterbrained at times, she was usually on time.

Chapter 6

Adam had called Cheryl first thing in the morning. She'd talked to him briefly while lying in bed looking out her window. After that, she fell asleep again and might've slept for hours if it wasn't for the car alarm going off on the street outside. She rolled over and looked at the clock. She was late. There was no way she would make it to her meeting with Day and Adam on time. Still, it took all the strength and willpower she had to drag herself out of bed. Her head pounded, and her mouth felt like it had been stuffed full of cotton. Her tongue was thick, and if she hadn't known better, she would've sworn she had a hangover. She hadn't felt this way since she was in college. That was the only time she thought getting so wasted she couldn't remember anything was fun. At some point, it turned from fun into tragic. It was probably from watching what alcohol had done to Mark. At least at one time, that's how she felt. Now she knew Mark was always bad even before he drank too much. He was just good at hiding it. She'd never been good at hiding anything.

Even though she was late, she jumped into the shower, hoping to wake herself up. She set the water temperature a little bit cooler than she usually would, but she got out still feeling headachy and sluggish.

The party incident and the police showing up at her house

all seemed to happen countless times on a loop like some twisted version of Groundhog Day. She loved that movie but hated experiencing it, especially when it kept her up all night. Now she didn't know if the police had ever actually shown up at her house last night or if she'd imagined everything that happened.

Scrubbed, dressed, and achy, she dragged herself to Day's shop, stopping to pick up coffee for everyone on the way.

Adam pulled the door open for her. "Coffee!" He took a cup from the drink tray as she came in.

"Thank you. Exactly what I need." Day took another cup from the tray and took a sip of coffee before giving Cheryl a once over. "Are you okay? You look like you haven't slept."

Cheryl put the tray on the counter before picking up her cup. The coffee was exactly what she needed. She couldn't wait for the caffeine to kick in. "I didn't. It sounded like there was a party going on all night."

"Who was partying?" Adam took a sip from his cup.

"I don't know. I think a ghost is trying to get my attention. I want to forget about it right now." She pulled her hair over her shoulder and twisted one of her spiral curls. "Let's talk about Stephanie and Will."

"I tried looking into the history of the house, but like Stephanie said, it's new, and there doesn't seem to be much there." Day picked up her tablet from the counter and tapped the screen to wake it up. "It was built in 1994, and the people who owned it before were pretty unremarkable. I couldn't find much on them besides their names. They didn't live in the house long. It looks like only about two years. I thought that seemed like a short time, so I looked back further. There is an unusually long list of occupants for a house built in the nineties. It was sold every two to three years." Day turned the screen of the tablet toward Cheryl so she could see the property appraiser's site with a list of the dates the house was sold and the price.

"Nobody wants to stay in a haunted house." Adam stood behind her, looking over her shoulder at the tablet screen.

"They should have to disclose that to whoever buys the house from them. You know, like you have to disclose that there's been any significant termite damage or the house is on a sinkhole or something." Cheryl thought it was a good idea.

Day laughed. "You can't put 'haunted' down if someone asked if there's anything wrong with your home. First of all, the majority of the population doesn't believe in ghosts."

"I know, but it's good for the people who do believe to know there's something going on, don't you think?" Cheryl asked. "I'd want to know." She walked over to the comfy chair in the corner. It had been calling her name. "I hope you don't mind. I need to sit down."

"No problem." Day and Adam migrated over to the corner to be close to Cheryl as they continued to talk. Day perched on the arm of the chair, and Adam stood awkwardly with his hands in his pockets.

"I have a folding chair in the back." Day stood.

Adam shook his head. "That's okay. I'm fine standing."

"I should get it." Day hurried to the back room.

"I had a rough night too," Adam said as they waited.

"A party?" Cheryl wondered if this would be a trend, and the same ghosts that were contacting her would try to contact him now.

"No. I think it had something to do with Stephanie and Will's case. I kept seeing the forest and wildlife walking around." He took another sip of his coffee.

Day came out carrying a dented, white folding chair. "It's not pretty, but it works."

Adam set his coffee on the bookshelf so he could set up

the chair. "Thanks." It creaked as he sat in it. "It was like I was in the wilderness preserve near their house. There was a coyote with only one eye."

"Poor coyote," Cheryl said.

"No, not like that. I mean it had one eye in the middle of its forehead. It never had two eyes."

"Oh, creepy." Cheryl looked at Day. "Any ideas about what that means?"

"Is that what you were talking about before when you were telling me about being a visionary?" Day asked.

"Yeah," he said.

Day pursed her lips and looked up for a moment as if trying to recall something. "I had a teacher once, years ago, who told me that fairy creatures look deformed."

"So you're saying that I'm seeing fairies." There was an edge in his voice that let them know he didn't believe in any such thing.

Day shrugged. "I don't know what you're seeing, but if it's helping, it must be a good thing, right?"

Adam nodded reluctantly.

"Did this coyote tell you anything about Stephanie and Will's house?" The coyote was interesting, but Cheryl was desperately looking for clues.

"No, it was a coyote. It didn't talk." His snarky tone annoyed her. She was too tired for this.

"How am I supposed to know that? You just told us that it had one eye in the middle of its forehead. Maybe it talked. How do I know?" Cheryl snapped.

Day changed the subject. "I'm working on contacting one of the previous owners of the house." Day settled back onto the arm of the chair and sipped her coffee. "I'm hoping someone will talk to me and tell me why they sold so quickly."

"That's a good idea." A sound rose in Cheryl's head. The

pulse of music that echoed what she'd heard from the night before pushed out her thoughts. A crowd cheered. "Do you hear that?" She could tell by the confusion on both of their faces that neither Adam nor Day heard anything at all.

"What?" Adam asked.

"It sounds like a dance party."

Adam and Day glanced at each other.

"I don't hear any dance music," Day said.

Cheryl listened, wondering if the sounds of dance music and reveling partiers were going to follow her around everywhere now. "I can't take this." She let out an exasperated sigh.

Adam said something, but she couldn't quite hear what because the music rose in volume and in tempo. Suddenly a party appeared in front of her. A group of transparent people danced and cheered, filling the entire store. "They're here." She stood up from her chair.

"Who?" Adam looked around.

Cheryl walked through the crowd, weaving in and out of the bodies bouncing in time with the music. Even though she knew they weren't really there, she did her best to avoid bumping into them. They dressed like they were in a 1970s movie, all bellbottoms and polyester with giant Afros and feathered hair. They swung their hips and laughed, clapping over their heads in time to the throbbing rhythm of the disco music. The store seemed to melt away, and Cheryl was in the midst of a nightclub. The infectious music drew her in. She bobbed her head and raised her arms in the air, swinging them back and forth to the beat. She undulated her hips in the middle of the crowd. Her skirt swayed back and forth. She was tired, but somehow the music took over. She couldn't resist. It filled her up.

She recognized someone in the dancing crowd. The ghost

dressed all in black that she'd seen in her apartment building. He wasn't dancing like the rest but walked through the crowd as if searching for something. Cheryl kept her eyes on him as she hurried through the crowd in his direction. She felt like the energy of the music was enough to carry her away from her senses. She had to focus to kept sight of him and remember what she was doing. Then....

Pop! Pop! Pop!

The noise broke through the rhythm of the music. The beat that felt like it was carrying her dropped her with a merciless thud to the ground. She opened her eyes to see people yelling and running around her in a panic, pushing each other to the floor. Trampling over one another, they tried to find an exit. The man in black had disappeared among the confusion. The sharp sound of metal scraping against metal rose over the noise, and the ceiling rolled back like the top of a sardine can. A column of dark smoke poured in. It snaked through the room like a living creature on the hunt, chasing partygoers. Wrapping itself around its victims like a boa constrictor, it squeezed the life out of them before continuing on to the next person in its sights. Once engulfed they'd collapse to the floor as they gagged in pain. Cheryl watched in horror as the smoked singled out and suffocated individuals. A woman in shiny neon-green leggings ran in front of Cheryl, screaming until the smoke wound itself around her like a snake., and she fell breathless to the ground. Then the column of smoke coiled through the frantic crowd searching for its next mark. It was calculated, targeting some and leaving others to escape to safety. The man in black pushed through the panicked partygoers to the exit. She felt the need to follow him. She hurried forward, not wanting to lose sight of him. A chill ran through her, and she turned, looking behind her only to realize that the smoke creature was zeroing in on her. She stood frozen in time. Fear ripped into her, and she yelled. Someone grabbed her shoulder, their hand heavy and hot. Cheryl swung around only to see Adam.

"It's okay. It's okay." He looked into her eyes.

The scene melted away. Cheryl was back in Day's shop. The calming music floated in the sandalwood-scented air. She was surrounded by books and crystals.

"What happened?" Day stood next to Adam.

Cheryl shook her head. "I don't know. I was somewhere else."

"We saw. You were really dancing there for a minute." Adam grinned.

"I was, wasn't I?" She must have looked like a fool. She walked back over to the chair, picked up her cup of coffee, and took a few more sips. Her headache was raging now. "I was just transported to a big disco extravaganza." She threw her arms up and emphasized the word "extravaganza" for comedic effect.

"It looked like you were having a good time at first," Day said.

"You know how these things go though. They always happen for a reason, and that reason isn't good." Sometimes Cheryl wondered how many strange experiences she could have in a lifetime.

Adam was looking at her like he was trying to see something inside of her.

"I was until things got scary. I have to figure out what that's all about." None of that mattered at the moment. Because this vision kept happening to her, she knew she would need to solve it, but she was here to talk about Stephanie and Will. Their case took priority. "I'll deal with it when whoever needs my help gets me more information. We have to focus on the case at hand. Maybe we should--" Her phone rang. She grabbed her purse from the floor and fished it out. It was Stephanie's number, but when she picked up the phone, the person on the other end wasn't Stephanie.

Chapter 7

There was something under the vanity again. Stephanie heard it while she was brushing her teeth. She had spit the white foam into the bathroom sink just as the door clacked in front of her leg. She jumped back and wiped the toothpaste from her mouth with her arm. "Will!"

Will sat in the living room watching the news on television. He always watched the news. Stephanie didn't care for it because it made her sad.

She heard scratching, like something scrambling around inside the vanity. The door rattled. "Will!"

She could hear the drone of the anchorman's voice, but Will didn't answer. Her toothbrush still in hand, she stormed into the living room. "Did you hear me calling you?"

He looked over at her with a blank expression on his face. "You called me? I didn't hear anything."

"That's weird because I called pretty--" She stopped herself. She didn't want to argue. "There's something in the vanity again."

"And you want me to get it out?" His eyes sparkled.

"Please." She pleaded.

"I'll see what I can do." He stood and took his time walking across the living room, up the hallway to the bedroom, and then to the master suite's bathroom, shuffling his feet on the tile as he went. Sometimes Stephanie felt like he was reluctant to help her. His words said one thing and his actions another.

When they stepped into the bathroom, she immediately noticed that the vanity door was open about an inch. She gasped and put her hand over her mouth. "It got out!"

Will was unworried. He pulled the vanity door open and looked inside. It was still a mess. "There's nothing in here. Just like the last time." He sounded bored.

"Of course, there's nothing in there because it got out!" She stood on her tiptoes as if having as little of her feet as possible in contact with the floor would prevent whatever it was from biting her. She pictured a rat slinking along the wall, looking for food. "I can't believe it. It got out." She searched the room frantically. She needed to find whatever it was but, at the same time, was terrified to find whatever it was. Will stood watching her as she knelt on the floor to look under the bed. Nothing was there. They'd lived in the house for such a short time that not even dust bunnies had accumulated under the bed yet. She went to the closet. When she put her hand on the doorknob to open it, Will spoke, interrupting her panic.

"Nothing's going to be in the closet. The door is closed."

She yanked the door open anyway and walked inside. Lifting the hems of pants, skirts, and dresses to get a good look at the floor, she searched for it along the wall. "It has to be here someplace."

Will yawned. "Let me know if you find it. I'm going to finish watching the news."

Stephanie walked around the house, looking in corners and closets. She opened all the cabinets in the kitchen and even considered moving the refrigerator to look behind it. She found nothing, but vermin were sneaky. They had places to hide that you would never even guess.

By the time the news was over, she had checked every corner and every closet of every room. She found nothing, but that didn't mean there was nothing in the house.

Will switched off the television. He looked up, reaching his arms toward the ceiling in a big stretch. Scratching his belly, he yawned. "You haven't found anything yet?"

"No." Stephanie stood in the kitchen, trying to decide whether or not she was going to move the appliances to check behind them. She was exhausted.

He sauntered over to her and put his arms around her waist from behind. His breath was hot on her neck. "Are you coming to bed?"

"Yeah." But she was uncertain. If she went to bed without finding it, what would happen in the night?

"Let's go to bed." He wandered into the bathroom to brush his teeth and get ready for sleep.

She hurried around the house, checking the corners of rooms and turning off the lights she had left on. By the time she got to the bedroom, he was already in bed. The lamp on his side was off. On her side, the lamp emitted a soft yellow glow. He lay on his back, and she couldn't tell whether or not his eyes were open. She stood next to the bed, looking at the bathroom door. Maybe she should close it.

"Be brave," he said, his voice groggy.

"What do you mean?" She stared at the open door.

"Nothing came out of the vanity. Don't close the door like you did last night. Be brave. Nothing will happen." If only he were right.

**

Stephanie had a restless night's sleep. She kept waking up

in the night because she felt like something was crawling on her, but when she opened her eyes and looked around, there was nothing. She sat up in bed, the skin on her arms tingling. Scratching, she looked around the room. Will lay on his side with his back facing her, snoring loudly. She dared not wake him, but she swore there was something in the room. She slid out of bed, her feet sinking into the thick throw rug on the tile floor. She had bought a shaggy rug for the bedroom because the idea of walking on the cold tile in the middle of the night was so off-putting. She padded into the bathroom. The vanity's doors were still closed tight. She reached down and pulled one of the doors open quickly, jumping back as she did. There was nothing inside.

Standing in the bathroom doorway, she looked out into the bedroom. The crack in the curtains let in the silvery glow of moonlight. Something in the house wasn't right. She could feel it. Her heart rose to her throat, and the hair on her arms stood on end. The cool wind from the air conditioner vent blew directly on her. She walked past a snoring Will to the hallway. To her right, the guest room door was closed, and the hallway was completely dark. To her left, the smallest bit of light crept toward her from the living room. She headed in that direction because everything inside her told her to stay out of the guest room. Even though she was putting on a brave face by looking around the house alone in the darkness of the night, she wasn't that brave.

She tiptoed up the hall toward the living room. She could see the television hanging on the wall before she got to the end of the hallway and was surprised to see that it was on. The sound was muted, but a picture of a hole in the dirt somewhere was on the screen. Stephanie stood in the entryway to the living room for a moment. She remembered Will turning off the television. The living room had been completely dark when she went to bed.

She picked up the remote control from the sofa to turn off the television, but before she did, the video zoomed in, and the screen darkened. She watched with uneasy curiosity, barely able to make out the sides of the hole because the screen was so dark. Then the zooming stopped, and she swore she saw the outline of a teddy bear in the darkness. She turned up the volume, and white noise blared through the speakers. Fumbling with the buttons, she nearly dropped the remote before managing to turn the television off. The room was cloaked in darkness. Only the moonlight trickled in the sliding glass door.

She stood in front of the sofa, looking at the black screen of the television and wondering what she had just seen. She was turning to put the remote control back on the arm of the sofa when the flash of something on the television screen caught her eye. The reflection of the top half of a woman's narrow face appeared in the lower corner of the screen. Stephanie gasped and spun around, expecting to see someone standing behind her, but there was no one. Only the sofa in the blank wall above it looked back at her. Her heart beating in her throat, she turned around, and the woman's reflection was still there, her face crawling with insects. The worms that formed her mouth moved, and words lurched out of her. "Beware," she warned, her voice a chorus of whispers.

Stephanie didn't hesitate. She spun around and ran to the bedroom. "Will!" Even though she was yelling, somehow he didn't wake up. Stephanie slammed the bedroom door closed and locked it, certain the woman had crawled out of the television and was after her even now. "Get up!"

He shifted in his sleep and groaned, but still, he didn't wake.

She ran toward the bed, and as she did, she heard

something. She froze and listened to the scraping sounds accompanied by a high-pitched squeal. She grabbed her phone from the bedside table and activated the flashlight app. She was terrified but wanted to know what was making that noise. It sounded like it was coming from beneath the bed. So, she bent down, getting on her hands and knees to find the source of the noise. At first, when she shined her flashlight under the bed, she saw nothing. The noise stopped, and an eerie silence hovered around her. Will had even stopped snoring. She moved the light to and fro beneath the bed until she saw it, a mass of dark flesh pulsating in the far corner under the spot where Will slept. It undulated almost as if it were made of jelly. Coarse, wiry hairs stuck out from it in every direction. It stretched out slowly, revealing its shape, a soft blob with long tapering insect legs. The thing turned to look at her, revealing its face. Her own pointed chin, prominent nose, and wide thin mouth looked back at her. Black hollow holes were where the eyes should be. Stephanie froze with fear as the thing began to squeak again. It stretched its neck before scuttling toward her so quickly there was no time to react.

He lay in bed, sleeping. His mouth opened slightly, sucking in life-giving oxygen. Stephanie stood over him, watching in the darkness. His face tilted away from her, exposing his vulnerable neck. Sleep was so strange, the way it left you defenseless. It would be so easy for someone to pounce on you and take your life while you were occupied in dreamland. What would that be like? Stephanie bent over Will. His dark hair stood up on one side. He snored just a little bit. His bare stomach rose and fell with each breath.

She held a tentative hand in front of his nose, feeling the

air. Inhale. Exhale. Inhale. Exhale. What if she made it stop?

He didn't know what that would feel like yet, but she knew, and she wanted to share that knowledge with him. Didn't he deserve as much? Wouldn't he want to see the darkness that waits for all of us?

She was still only thinking about everything she could do to him when the sun came up. She'd been crouched beside the bed watching for hours, unsure of how to proceed. A beam of light came into the room through a slit in the curtains casting an orange glow. She watched the column of light move across the room as the morning ticked away.

Will's eyes flew open. "Steph, what's wrong?" He was breathless. Was he afraid of her? How funny was that?

She blinked at him blankly.

He sat up. "What are you doing?"

She shrugged but said nothing.

"Are you okay?" She sat back on the floor, hugging her knees to her chest. "Steph?"

When she didn't answer, he moved to the floor, wrapping his arms around her. She felt like he was consuming her. He was swallowing her up, and there was nothing she could do. She hummed a song, a simple melody her mother used to sing and continued to rock back and forth. The bug lady told her she could be strong, but that wasn't true. She would never be strong enough. Even now, she was too small.

**

They left as soon as Will called. His panicked tone terrified Cheryl.

"What did he say?" Day asked in the car. She drove because she was excited to show off her new silver-blue BMW. It had been her dream car, and she finally got it.

Cheryl had never been impressed by cars, but she had to admit the idea of getting something this nice one day was appealing. She couldn't trust her 1996 Pontiac that was more rust than paint. She could barely trust the old beater to start in the morning, let alone to get her where she needed to go. She felt lucky that it hadn't broken down by the side of the road, leaving her in a precarious situation.

Day had already commented on how smooth the ride was five times since they left St. Pete. "He just said she was acting strange. He didn't tell me how, but he sounded like it was an emergency. She might be possessed."

"Before I started this job, if anyone would've asked me," Adam said, "I would've said that possession wasn't real. I would've told them that people don't get possessed. They have mental health issues that need treatment. That's not the case at all. I've seen so many possessions since we started."

"Remember when I told you about how, if your life is kind of a mess, it makes you more susceptible to hauntings?" Cheryl asked him.

"I think the same thing is true of your mind. Demons start to weaken you by making you feel confused and scared. That's how they can crawl inside of you." Cheryl spoke with conviction, but in reality, she knew just about as much as Adam did. Every experience that she had professionally with ghosts, he had been there for.

"Stephanie always seemed together to me." Day stepped down on the accelerator to pass a pickup truck blowing out black clouds of exhaust.

"Stephanie's good at looking together, but in reality, she isn't." Cheryl knew. Stephanie was insecure, always wondering if she was behind in life. Cheryl knew the feeling; she often wondered too. She wasted so much time with Mark that she felt like she was underwater more than just financially. She always told herself that any experience had its benefits, but she didn't know how true that necessarily was.

"What was she doing that was so strange?" Adam asked from the back seat.

"I'm not sure. He didn't explain. He just wants us to come." Adam and Day bantered back and forth as Cheryl sat in the front seat, looking out the window, imagining the worst. Every case they had seemed to have increasingly bigger stakes and this one felt particularly big to Cheryl. While their last case was about finding closure and finally putting to rest all of the terrible consequences Mark had created in this world, this case was about Cheryl's present. Stephanie had meant so much to her life since she had moved to town. She had been so grateful to find a friend so quickly, and one as loyal and understanding as Stephanie was rare. She couldn't let anything happen to her. She wouldn't.

Chapter 8

Will and Stephanie were standing in the driveway when they pulled up. Adam sat forward in the back seat to get a good look at them. They stood in front of the house hand-in-hand.

"She looks fine," Adam said as Day turned off the car.

"Looks can be deceiving." Day opened the driver's side door. "So, what's going on?" she asked them.

Cheryl made a beeline for Stephanie. "Are you okay? How do you feel?"

Stephanie shrugged. "Will said I was acting strange, but honestly, I don't remember. I feel fine."

"You feel fine now, but when I woke up, you were on the floor next to the bed crying." He turned his attention to Cheryl. "She wouldn't talk to me or tell me what was wrong. I panicked." Will put his arm around Stephanie's shoulders. "I'm sorry to make you drive all the way down here for nothing."

"How did things go during the night, Stephanie?" Something didn't seem right to Adam, but he couldn't quite put his finger on what it was. "Did you see or hear anything strange?"

Stephanie shook her head. "I slept well. That hasn't been happening recently."

"Really?" Cheryl glanced at Adam.

"Yeah." Stephanie was sure to make eye contact with each of them. "I slept like a baby."

"Well, since we're here, we should take a look at the footage from last night just to see if anything unusual showed up." Adam motioned to the front door.

"Sure, come on in." Will held the door open for all of them to go inside.

Day and Cheryl sat down in the living room on the sofa while Adam went to the first camera that was pointed out the sliding glass doors to see if they caught anything. He fast-forwarded through a lot of footage of trees waving in the wind and opossums and raccoons scurrying by before getting to anything interesting. The final video started with the fence in the back garden vanishing. In one frame of the video, it was there, and, in the next, it was gone. Once it disappeared, beyond the fence line stood a wilderness much lusher than the one currently there. Large prehistoric-looking ferns reached into their backyard. The forest moved and swayed as if it were alive. "Look at this." He waved for everyone to join him around the screen. They all pressed together, looking over his shoulder at the tiny grainy image just as some animals came into view.

A wave of woodland creatures clambered over each other into the garden--squirrels, rabbits, raccoons, opossums, mice, and rats. They swarmed over the grass, covering it completely, and surged forward onto the patio. A single raccoon came close to the glass pressing its hands against it and looking right into the camera lens. Even though the image was grainy, it was so close that its face was perfectly clear, revealing that instead of two eyes, he had one. It blinked slowly in the middle of its forehead just above its snout.

"Oh my god, are you seeing what I'm seeing?" Cheryl asked. She squeezed Adam's shoulder.

Of course, Adam saw it. Everyone did. But unlike everyone, he was calm because he had seen it before.

"Why does it only have one eye?" Day asked.

"That was going on outside while we were sleeping?" The air had gone out of Will's voice.

"Apparently." Adam didn't know what else to say.

The raccoon stared into the camera for what seemed like ages. Adam couldn't pull his gaze from its hypnotic eye. Then the glass it pressed its hand against began to move. Someone was opening the sliding glass door. The raccoon turned to face the other animals behind before hurrying into the house.

"They came inside?" Will's voice rose as he looked around the living room. "How is that possible? I didn't hear anything last night. Did you hear anything?" He turned to Stephanie, who shook her head.

She looked off to the side before speaking. "I didn't hear anything at all." Her speech was slower than normal.

"That can't be true." Will's voice was sharp with accusation. "You know what happened last night. That's why you were acting so strange this morning." He pointed at her.

Adam handed the camera to Cheryl before going over to look at the other camera pointed into the living room. He watched the screen alone. There were a couple of videos of nothing. It must've been activated by a fly or a small insect. But the fourth video got interesting.

Stephanie came into view. She stepped out of the hallway in a short nightgown. She stood in front of the television for a few minutes staring at the dark screen, her body swaying back and forth ever so slightly. Then she turned and walked across the living room with her head angled oddly. She looked up and to the left, not in the direction she was walking. Her movements were almost mechanical as she crept across the living room. She went straight to the sliding glass doors.

Standing there for a moment, she looked outside. The glass doors were visible at the edge of the screen, and Adam could see that as soon as she arrived, the raccoon came to the door, pressing its front paws against the glass. She looked down at the raccoon before nodding and pulling the door open. When she did, the animals rushed in, piling on top of her as she fell backward onto the floor. Then the video cut off. Adam looked at Stephanie, who stood next to Will watching the other video with Cheryl and Day, but she wasn't looking at the screen. She seemed to be looking down too far and slightly over at the floor next to where the camera was. Her body was unnaturally stiff and her hands were balled into fists.

"What is it?" Day was staring at him. She broke free from the others and walked over to join him.

Adam didn't know why, but his instinct was to hide the video. He had the distinct feeling that if Stephanie knew what was on it, she would do something bad. Quickly, before Day reached his side, he cued up one of the other videos, one where the camera had turned on because of a moth. "There's nothing here." He pushed play on the video so Day could look at the empty room with him.

"That's impossible. We just saw all the animals go inside on the other video." Day pointed to the other camera. "Where could they have gone?"

Cheryl joined them. Adam hoped when she looked down at the screen, she wouldn't notice how many other videos there were. He hoped she wouldn't want to scroll through them herself but that she would take him for his word. "Nothing on any of these videos. It looks like they're just triggered by insects."

Holding the other camera down at her side, she pressed up next to him. She put her hand on his back as she looked down at the screen and watched the video he played for her. "I don't understand."

"Does that surprise you?" He lowered the camera by his side quickly before she had a chance to notice the other videos.

"None of this makes sense." Will looked into Stephanie's eyes, but she looked away.

"It doesn't," she whispered.

"Let's check the other cameras anyway." Cheryl set the camera she was carrying on the bar and walked over to the one they had pointed into the hallway.

Adam's heart started to thump. Stephanie would be on this video too, but he didn't want her to know. Adam hurried over to Cheryl as she reached out to take the camera off the tripod. "Can we talk outside for a minute?"

Cheryl looked at him with questioning eyes. "Let's look at the video, and then we can talk on the way home."

Adam looked over at Day. "I need to talk to you alone for a minute. It won't take long."

She hesitated. "Okay."

Before they went outside, Adam grabbed the camera still on the tripod and carried it with him out into the front door. He couldn't risk one of them deciding to look at the video without them.

**

Adam grabbed Cheryl's arm and pulled her outside with an urgency that made her nervous. "What's wrong?" she asked.

Adam peered inside at Will, Stephanie, and Day, who were

all looking at them. "We'll be back in a minute." Then he shut the door.

"What's on the video?" Cheryl looked down at the cameras, one slung over his shoulder by the strap, and the other one in his hand still attached to the tripod.

He lowered his voice and stepped in closer to her. "It's Stephanie. She opens the glass doors and lets those animals in."

"No way." Cheryl couldn't imagine why Stephanie would do such a thing.

"Look." He put down the camera that was still on the tripod and lifted the one hanging from the strap dangling over his shoulder. He scrolled to the video and pressed play.

Cheryl was aware that he was looking at her the whole time she watched the video, waiting for her response. She couldn't believe what she was seeing. "Oh my goodness!" She looked back at the front door where Stephanie, Will, and Day stood inside. "What's with all these animals? I don't understand." The thought of all of those animals crawling all over Stephanie gave Cheryl shivers. What were they doing? What did it all mean? "What's on the other camera?" She nodded toward the camera on the tripod sitting on the ground next to him.

"Let's find out." Picking it up, he began scrolling through the videos. Then he picked one and pressed play. Cheryl moved closer to him so she could get a good look at the video too. On it, she saw exactly what she expected. Stephanie, looking just like she did in the previous video, walked up the hallway and into the living room. The person in the video looked just like Stephanie, but the way she moved was different. It was all wrong. "She has to be possessed. There is no other explanation."

"Which means she's possessed now," Adam said what she

had been thinking.

"But she's acting so normal." Cheryl knew just as well as anyone that that meant nothing. Will, after all, had called to say that Stephanie was acting strangely. He was obviously worried.

"I wanted to show this to you before we showed it to anyone else because I wasn't sure what to do." Adam played the video of Stephanie walking down the hallway again, but Cheryl didn't bother to look at it. She had seen enough.

"We have to show her and ask her if she remembers it." Cheryl was winging it, of course, like she always was. She didn't know why Adam liked to defer to her. He knew as much about any of this as she did. Sometimes she thought he might know more. She didn't have the time to study between working for the psychic network, doing tarot card readings, and all the worrying she did about the bills she needed to pay.

"Do we want whatever is inside of her to know that we know?" He was still looking at the video.

"Yes. We need Stephanie and Will to know. We also need whatever's inside of her to know. So we can get rid of it." That uneasy feeling crept across Cheryl again. She swallowed hard and crossed her arms over her chest, suddenly feeling a bit chilly despite the afternoon heat.

"Are you okay?" he asked her.

Cheryl nodded. "I'm not going to let Stephanie down."

"No one said you would."

She looked at the front door, thinking about Stephanie. "Let's go inside and tell them what's going on." The steady beat of disco rose in her thoughts. Cheryl rolled her eyes. "Not now," she said to the sky.

"What?" Adam asked, his hand already on the doorknob.

"Just the disco again, but they're not going to bother me now because I'm working on an important case." She continued looking skyward. The music stopped as suddenly as it started. "Thank you." She looked at Adam. "It's gone. Let's go talk to whatever is inside of Stephanie."

Chapter 9

"I don't understand." Stephanie watched the video playback in front of her. What she saw made no sense at all. The person in the video looked like her, but it couldn't be her. She watched herself leave the bedroom, walk down the hallway, and let a bunch of wild animals into their house, but she didn't remember doing any such thing. She knew she never would've done that. Never in a million years. She looked around the living room where they stood and saw no evidence of animals there. Everything around them was clean and intact. The whole space looked just like it had before they'd gone to bed the previous night. Even more disturbing than seeing herself walk up the hallway looking like she was possessed was what happened after she opened the sliding glass doors. She shuddered at the idea of all those animals crawling over her. Opossums, raccoons, rats, squirrels... There were so many that she couldn't identify them all. What were they doing to her? She looked down at her arms for evidence of bite marks or scratches. Nothing. Her skin was smooth and unblemished.

When the video ended, she looked over at Will, who was staring at her suspiciously. "What did you do?" He narrowed his eyes at her.

Suddenly Stephanie felt like she was the bad guy. "I don't know. I don't remember anything." He had to believe her. "It's just like the time you caught me sleepwalking in the backyard."

He shook his head. "No, it's not. Then you were just sleepwalking. This is something else."

Cheryl played the video again, and they all gathered closer to watch. Stephanie could only look at the first section. Seeing herself looking like an empty husk floating by on the screen was too much. She broke out of the huddle of people and began to pace.

Cheryl handed the camera to Adam and went over to her. "Let's talk alone."

Stephanie looked out the sliding glass doors. There was no way she would go into the backyard. They wandered up the hallway to the guest room. It was a mess, but there were a couple of chairs they could sit in. Stephanie pushed the door open and motioned for Cheryl to walk in. She followed close behind, expecting to sit and explain to Cheryl that she had no idea what was happening, but nothing in this house was that simple.

**

Stephanie gasped and held her hand over her mouth. "How did you get in here?" She stepped back toward the doorway. "Can you see her?"

Cheryl saw her. A young girl, who looked to be no older than six stood in the far corner of the room behind a stack of boxes. She wore a red satin dress and only one shoe. Her dark hair was combed into a smooth bob. The teddy bear dangled from her hand by its leg, its ears nearly brushing the floor. Cheryl squatted in front of her. "Hello. I'm Cheryl. What's your name?"

The girl shook her head, her hair lightly hitting her chin. She pressed her tiny lips together, letting Cheryl know that she didn't intend to speak.

"That's her. That's the girl I saw before." Stephanie was still moving backward.

Cheryl whipped her head around to look at Stephanie. "I know you're scared, but you need to calm down. We don't want to scare her."

Stephanie's chest rose and fell, her breath wheezing.

Cheryl knew she needed someone to comfort her, but she couldn't do it now. She had to pay attention to the girl to find out who she was and what she knew. "What's your name?" She turned her attention back to the girl.

The child moved her mouth like she was speaking, but no words came out.

Stephanie rushed out of the room. Cheryl could hear her feet on the tile going down the hallway. "She's here! That little girl is here!"

"What did you say, dear?" Cheryl leaned in closer to the girl. "I can't hear you." She smelled of soil.

The girl pressed her lips together and looked down at the floor.

"It's okay. You're safe here." Cheryl reached out her hand to touch the girl's arm, but before she could, Adam and Will appeared in the doorway.

"Where is she?" Will asked, a note of fear in his voice.

Stephanie was right behind them. "I told you she was real."

Cheryl had turned around to look at them. "Don't be afraid," she said as she turned back to the girl. Cheryl froze when she saw that the girl was no longer there. In her place, an opossum stood in the corner, its mouth open bearing two rows of pointed white teeth. It hissed, and Cheryl realized her outstretched hand was only inches from its mouth. She could feel its hot breath on her fingers. Slowly, she withdrew her hand. The opossum turned its head back and forth as if trying to make sure she got a full view of its teeth.

"Where did that come from?" Will asked.

"Cheryl, be careful!" Adam froze in the doorway. "It's going to bite you."

She took her time rising to her full height. She didn't want to scare it with any sudden movements. Once she stood up completely, the opossum looked up at her with its black marble-like eyes. Cheryl swore she saw panic in its face before it passed out. It lay on the floor perfectly still with its mouth still gaping open, showing its teeth.

"It fainted." Day came up behind everyone. "Do you have something we can wrap it in to carry it outside?"

"Yeah." Will disappeared up the hall.

"What happened to the girl?" Stephanie pushed past Adam into the room. "Where is the girl?"

Cheryl was wondering the same thing. "I don't know. She was right here." Cheryl pointed at the opossum.

Will rushed into the room, holding a towel and wearing a pair of suede work gloves. The fingers were so thick that they made his hands look deformed. "Can I just pick it up?"

"Yeah," Day said. "It will stay out of it as long as it's scared."

He made quick work of wrapping the opossum in the towel, being sure to cover its mouth and eyes. Then he took it into the front yard and laid it in the grass. All but Stephanie followed him. She stayed in the spare room, walking in circles as if performing a ritual.

Once the opossum was safely outside, Cheryl returned to the doorway of the room to check on Stephanie, who was walking around the room, muttering to herself and swinging her arms. She seemed like a different person to Cheryl at that moment. She definitely wasn't the put-together friend who alphabetized the books on her shelves who Cheryl had come to know over the years. That woman wouldn't walk in circles in a room checking the same corner again and again for something that obviously wasn't there.

"Are you okay?"

Upon hearing her voice, Stephanie froze. She looked over at Cheryl with a blank look on her face. "What?" She shook her head as if trying to shake something off. "Did you say something?"

"Yeah." Cheryl stepped into the room and closed the door. She wondered where the others were. Maybe they were still outside watching the opossum, waiting to see if it would wake up and walk away. Where would it go in the middle of the day? Weren't they only supposed to be out at night? For a moment, she found herself forgetting that the opossum had been a little girl a few moments earlier and worrying for its safety. She needed to stop thinking about the opossum. She was dealing with Stephanie now. "Are you okay? You keep walking in circles."

Stephanie looked around the room as if realizing where she was. "Was I?" She sat down on the bed.

"Do you remember what just happen?"

She looked up and to the right, pursing her lips. It took a moment for her to answer. "Could you remind me?"

Cheryl closed her eyes and let out a sigh. She sat on the bed next to her. "Tell me what you remember."

"You all came here because Will called. He said I'd been acting weird. The last I remember, we were going to look at the videos to see if the cameras captured anything interesting last night." She spoke slowly as if remembering took a lot of effort.

"That's it? You don't remember anything after that?" Cheryl looked into Stephanie's eyes to see if she could see anything that seemed different.

She shook her head.

"What about last night?"

Stephanie thought for a moment. "I remember going to bed."

"But not getting up in the middle of the night and walking around the house." Cheryl was hoping that something had shifted in Stephanie, and more memories would begin peeking through.

Adam opened the bedroom door. "The opossum's gone."

Cheryl didn't know if that was a good thing or not. Should they have kept it?

He looked at Stephanie, who had a look of confusion on her face. "What's going on in here?" He stepped into the room.

"Stephanie doesn't remember anything after we arrived."

Stephanie bounced her knee up and down nervously.

Cheryl placed her hand on it to stop it. "It's going to be okay." She reassured her.

"Is it?" Stephanie stood, pushing Cheryl's hand off her leg. "I don't remember last night or this morning. How can I be okay?"

"You're right. But do you feel like yourself right now?" Cheryl stood and put her hand on the upper part of Stephanie's back just between her shoulder blades.

"Yes." She closed her eyes and paused as if reconsidering. Then she opened them again and said, "I guess I do." She looked at the floor. She bit her lip. "Kind of." Her eyebrows drew together in a scowl.

"What do you mean kind of?" Adam asked.

Will and Day had appeared in the doorway behind him now. "Yeah, what do you mean kind of?" Will narrowed his eyes at her as if looking for what she might be hiding.

"I don't know." Stephanie closed her eyes tight and

reached up with one hand to massage her temple. "Maybe I need to lie down for a little bit."

"Okay. You should rest if you need it. We're just going to get these videos off the cameras and set them up again, and then we'll be on our way," Cheryl said.

They all watched Stephanie carefully as she padded out of the room on bare feet. Cheryl watched her gait, looking for clues that she wasn't who she said she was. She walked normally though.

Adam changed the SD cards in the cameras so he could take them home and analyze the videos on them. There were a few times when the video was triggered, and it seemed like nothing was there. They wouldn't know if that was the case until they took a closer look, but they couldn't do that here.

They were getting ready to go when Will stopped them. "There's one thing we forgot to mention." He stood as if frozen, his eyebrows raised.

"Go on then," Day said.

"She keeps hearing something under the bathroom sink. It sounds like an animal, but every time we look, there's been nothing there. There is evidence something has been in there, like knocked down bottles and shredded toilet paper. Stephanie says she sees the door bouncing sometimes like something's trying to get out. I've checked the whole thing, and there's no way for anything to get in there. Not even the smallest crack."

Cheryl and Adam looked at each other. "We should go check it out."

Will let out a nervous laugh. "Wouldn't it be funny if there was a doorway to hell underneath our bathroom sink?"

Cheryl and Adam laughed too. "You'd be surprised by some of the stuff we've seen," Cheryl said. "We saw a bed eat someone once."

Will raised an eyebrow. "No kidding."

"I swear on my life." Cheryl raised her right hand as if taking an oath.

"We should take a look." Adam shut the car door.

"It's the one off the master bedroom, and Stephanie's lying down." Will looked back toward the house.

"We can check it out next time then." Cheryl pulled open the passenger side door.

"We'll go home and look at these videos and analyze what we have," Day said. "Then we'll get back to you."

Will nodded.

"Keep an eye on Stephanie." Adam opened the car door again.

"We'll be back soon," Cheryl said before they all got into the car.

As Day backed out of the driveway, she said, "So what do you think?"

"I'm not sure what to think." Cheryl adjusted the air conditioning vent, so it blew directly on her even though the air was still hot. "Something is definitely not right with Stephanie."

"There's probably more in these videos than we saw at the house." Adam looked at the SD card, a small plastic square in his hand.

"We'll see," Cheryl said. "We'll see."

Chapter 10

As Stephanie lay in the bed staring at the ceiling, she could hear Day, Cheryl, Adam, and Will talking, but it didn't take her long to drift off into another world. As soon as she closed her eyes, she felt herself falling like Alice down the rabbit hole. Her heart rose into her throat, and she felt weightless. In that kind of dream, most never land; they tumble downward until waking, but Stephanie landed in a field of lime-green grass that stretched up toward the sky. Even though she had hit the ground hard, she felt no pain. She landed in a sitting position, her legs stretched out in front of her. She blinked, her eyes adjusting to the bright sunlight. After the initial shock of landing, she noticed the noise. The wind whooshed in her ears. Everywhere around her she could hear clicking, tapping, and chewing. Animals chattered and squeaked. Looking down in the grass where she sat, she saw a row of tiny black ants marching along the dirt and swore she could hear each of their tiny footsteps. They moved in time like a marching band in a parade. Birds whistled, chirped, and screeched. Their squawks were so loud they hurt her ears. So much was coming at her that it was hard to take it all in. Stephanie covered her ears with her hands, trying to block out some of the noise that pummeled her. She pulled her legs up to her chest and buried her face in her knees. She pressed her hands against her ears as hard as she could.

"Stop it! Stop it!" She yelled into her legs. "Be quiet!" She wondered how long it would be before she would wake up and be free of the loud nightmare. Even though it was a dream, she was aware of her sleeping self lying in bed. "Shut up!" She yelled as loud as she could. As if obeying her command, everything went silent. The noise melted away, and the world around her stopped like someone had pressed pause. The wind disappeared. The grass stopped mid-sway. The ants froze as if playing a game of red light, green light. The world that was so loud before plunged into silence. With wide eyes, Stephanie looked around her. She stood. Dusting the dirt off her pants, she looked toward the trees. Should she go into the forest?. Was it safe there? She had no way of knowing. That same uneasy feeling that she felt in her backyard had settled in the center of her chest. It pushed into her, making it difficult to take a deep breath. How long would it be before she woke up? Was this really still a dream? If it was, why did it feel so real?

Her senses seemed to amplify until she could hear the beating of her heart... thump, thump like a drum. The blood rushed through her veins in rhythmic pulses. The sounds from her body had become so loud that she almost wished for the outside noise to return. Then among the stillness, she saw something, movement in the trees and a flash of color. It took a few moments for her to make it out. A woman walked toward her in a long, yellow dress. She stepped from among the dense shrubbery of the forest to reveal herself. Chipmunks, squirrels, and raccoons scurried around her feet, circling her ankles. An opossum perched on her shoulders. Its bald tail curled around her neck. Her mahogany skin seemed to be made from the earth itself. The outline of leaves and the texture of bark defined her muscles. Dark, twisting vines and tendrils of Spanish moss hung from her scalp instead of hair. She walked slowly, and so smoothly it was almost as if she was gliding just above the ground.

Stephanie's instincts told her to run, but turning her back on the woman could only result in disaster. She took large clumsy steps backward in the tall grass, keeping her eyes on the woman walking purposefully toward her.

"Get away from me! Leave me alone!" Stephanie took another step back and another. Finally, in a panic, she turned to run, but as she did, her ankle twisted, and she fell, driving her hands into the dirt. Grass stained her knees. She turned around to see the woman standing over her. Her eyes were black holes looking down at Stephanie. The woman's skin was alive with insects. Ants and beetles crawled up her arms. Roaches scurried over each other on her neck too. An earthworm crawled out of one nostril and wiggled its way down to her mouth. She parted her lips slightly and let it crawl inside, disappearing into the dark hole.

Stephanie swallowed her disgust and somehow managed to push down her fear. "What do you want?"

The opossum slept on the woman's shoulder. It's nose pointed downward as it rested its head. The animals at her feet were more active now. They tore around her ankles, ripping up grass and sending chunks of dirt into the air. They moved so quickly that Stephanie could barely see what they were until one stopped. A squirrel froze, looking up at Stephanie with one hypnotic black eye in the center of its head. She couldn't look away.

The animal opened its mouth, revealing a row of dagger-like teeth. Its dark eyes went red as fire, and it lunged toward her, snarling and twisting its face with anger.

Stephanie crab-walked backward.

The woman snapped, and specks of dirt fell from her

fingertips to the ground. The squirrel looked up at her, its mouth still open. She shook her head, and the squirrel closed its mouth once again, hiding its fangs, and returned to running around her ankles with the others.

The woman leaned over Stephanie as if trying to get a closer look at her through her nonexistent eyes. Stephanie let out a yell, loud and shrieking. She sat up and found herself in her bedroom, the afternoon light streaming in through the window.

The door burst open, and Will stood there. "What is it? Are you okay?"

"I'm fine. It was just a bad dream." The woman's face, her skin undulating with life, and her hollow black eyes were burned into Stephanie's memory. It may have been a dream, but it felt real, and Stephanie couldn't imagine ever being able to rid herself of the woman's frightening image again.

**

They gathered around the counter in Day's shop to watch the videos together. There was so much more to sort through, but they wanted to look at what they'd already seen and talk more freely than they did back at the house.

Cheryl looked at the ominous footage of Stephanie walking up the hallway. She seemed devoid of the personality that Cheryl had come to know all these years. When her face turned away from the camera, it was easy to imagine it wasn't Stephanie at all.

"The woman made from bugs that you saw last time didn't show up again?" Adam asked her.

"No." Cheryl thought it was strange that the bug woman

hadn't made another appearance. Ghosts almost always showed up when she was around.

"You didn't see anything around Stephanie?" Day walked away from the counter and stuck her hands into the pockets of her slacks. "I felt something there today. It's strange because sometimes I do, and sometimes I don't. The first time you came by the house, I didn't feel anything, but you saw things. This time you didn't see anything, but I felt something." She enunciated the word "something" like it was important.

"What did you feel?" Adam had stopped the video now, and Cheryl continued to look at the frozen image of Stephanie standing in the hallway mid-stride, looking up at the ceiling, her neck tilted at an unusual angle.

"I don't know if I can even explain it. I guess it's something like Stephanie described, a rising sense of dread. I don't just feel it in the backyard. It's all over the house. I feel it as soon as I get out of the car. It sent shivers through me today. It takes a minute to adjust." Day looked up at the ceiling for a moment before returning her gaze to Adam. "Before you guys came, I tried everything. I tried spells and smudging and surrounding the house with a line of salt. I put bowls of uncooked rice on the windowsills and made rosemary wreaths. Nothing worked." Day built her techniques on the backs of ancestors. She relied on folk magic and traditions. Cheryl had once relied on the same until, just by chance, she fell into something much more direct. Spells, concoctions, and mojo bags worked though. She'd witnessed their workings for herself. She would continue to do that kind of work as long as she saw the need for it, but now she could augment it with something much more powerful. Day let out a heavy sigh, pulling Cheryl back into what she was saying. "I was having a hard time figuring out whether or not anything was really going on."

Day continued to talk, but Cheryl's attention was drawn away by the rhythm of a bass drum. Music swelled. "You don't hear that?" She interrupted Day midsentence.

"Is the music back?" Adam asked.

Cheryl nodded her head before a blanket of sound fell over her, and she was in the midst of a dance party. People gyrated and bounced to the music all around her. The scene was all too familiar, but this time, she would not let the music overtake her. She needed to see what happened. The rest of the world dropped away, and she was in another place, another time. The music vibrated in the walls of her chest. As she scanned the crowd, one person caught her attention. A small, brown-skinned woman with her black hair pulled into a side ponytail, wearing shiny, mustard-yellow leggings and a sparkling teal top. She danced with gusto, flinging her arms in the air and pumping her hips from side to side. Though her movements were one of someone having fun, she had a pained look in her eyes, and her square jaw was set. Her lips turned downward in a frown. As she danced, she looked around the room, turning her focus from one person to the next.

This was the woman Cheryl was meant to see, but why? The only way to know was to speak to her. Cheryl pushed her way through the crowd. "Excuse me. Pardon me," she said as she went. Her words were useless. The music was too loud. Surprisingly, the people, though only seen in some sort of vision, seemed to be flesh and blood. She felt their bodies bump against her as she went, but it was as if they didn't feel her. No one missed a beat in their dancing. No one made a move to avoid her. A man spun around, stretching out his arm and smacking her in the nose. The impact was so shocking she almost fell. He didn't turn to look at her or apologize. He continued to dance. Cheryl bent over with her hand over her nose. Suddenly the music dropped away and faded into Adam's voice.

"Are you okay?" he asked.

"Here take these." Day shoved the box of tissues in front of her face.

Cheryl looked down, realized that she was bent over in the bookstore with hot, red blood gushing from her throbbing nose. She grabbed some tissues and held them up to her nostrils, tilting her head back. She could taste the blood in her throat like a handful of pennies. She swallowed, trying to get rid of the metallic taste, and pinched her nose shut.

"Sit down and keep your head back." Day's hand was on her elbow, guiding her to the chair in the corner.

"I don't want to get blood on your chair."

"Don't worry about it." Day nearly shoved her down onto the chair.

It didn't take long for her nose to stop bleeding. While she sat there with her head back, Day and Adam buzzed about her, asking questions, but Cheryl was lost in her own world. She had never experienced being physically touched by a ghost. How was this possible?

Chapter 11

Adam was up late, pouring over videos. They seemed to have an impossible amount of footage from Stephanie and Will's house. He'd looked at the videos of Stephanie wandering the house a few more times on his own, searching for more clues. Once he decided there was nothing else to see, he continued to the others. Many contained nothing but the still image of an empty room. The camera must have been set off by something small, an insect maybe. Occasionally he'd notice a fly looping clumsily in the air in front of the lens. He had looked through hours of footage, his eyelids drooping with fatigue when he pressed play on the final video. This one came from the camera that sat in the kitchen by the bar, pointed into the living room. The view included the couch and most of the wall behind it. On the side of the screen, a bit of the sliding glass doors was in view, where the camera was pointed outside to record the backyard's activity. Something streaked across the screen. It happened so fast that it registered as only a blip to Adam. At first, he thought it might have been a glitch in the video, but his instinct told him to play it again. He did. Something was there. Slowing down the video, he could make out what it was. A little girl in a party dress with dark hair skipped happily across the screen. He couldn't see her face, only the side of her head. She was small and had to be the child Stephanie told them about. He ran the video back and played it again. The girl skipped across the screen again with her head slightly down, so the curtain of her hair hid her profile. She headed from the hallway to the sliding glass doors in the living room. She was already in the house, but where?

Adam looked at the time. It was late, maybe too late to call Cheryl. She had needed to sleep, and the video would still be there in the morning. He put his phone down and decided not to   call.

**

Stephanie woke because the house was unusually cold. She shivered beneath the cotton sheet. Rolling over, she reached out her arm, expecting to feel Will next to her, but he was gone, and the space on the mattress where he should've been was ice cold. The air conditioner heaved out chilly air at an alarming rate. Assuming he was in the bathroom, she rolled over, but the bathroom door was shut tight with the towel shoved under it just like she'd left it. She sat up.

"Will?" she called into the darkness. She waited a few moments, listening for his answer from someplace else in the house. She only heard the mechanical grind of the air conditioner. She would turn it down, and then find Will.

She eased herself out of bed, her bare feet meeting the soft carpet. She immediately noticed the grit beneath her soles. Why was the carpet so dirty? She'd have to remember to vacuum in the morning. It wasn't until she reached the hallway that she realized there was a trail of dirt on the tile floor a few inches wide. The line of dark dirt stood out against the white tile. It led up the hallway into the living room. Her eyes trained on the line; she followed it. She tiptoed up the corridor and through the living room to the sliding glass door where the line abruptly came to an end. The outside light was off, and the world beyond the glass door was so dark she couldn't see anything. Dark clouds hovered overhead, blocking the light of the moon and stars. She heard a high-pitched squeal in the distance that seemed to be begging her to come outside. It drew her to it so that her internal organs seemed to shift forward with yearning.

Stephanie unlatched the sliding glass door. It glided soundlessly on its track as she pushed it open. Then she stepped outside. She didn't need a line of dirt to tell her where to go from here. She already knew. It was calling her, telling her   exactly   where   she   had   to   be.

**

Cheryl stood in her living room with her hands over her ears. She couldn't block out the noise, no matter how hard she tried. Her laptop sat on the coffee table, turned on. She had selected the first random movie she came across, a teenage rom-com from years ago. It blared from her laptop speakers so loudly that she knew that any minute a neighbor might knock on her door to complain. The relentless music in her head pounded steadily. Each time she closed her eyes, she could see the dancers in the club dressed in colorful polyester, laughing and gyrating to the music, unaware of what was about to happen to them.

It felt like it had been years since she had gotten a decent night's sleep. Her head ached just behind her eyes, and exhaustion muddled her thoughts. She didn't want to be awake, but she couldn't sleep either. She looked at Beau, who slept curled up on one of the chairs pushed beneath the dining table, how she envied him. She watched his stomach gently rise and fall as he dozed.

How many days would she have to endure this? Another

sleepless night would be enough to end her. The music in her head came to another crescendo. Delirious with fatigue, she stopped the movie on her computer and stormed into the bedroom. She pulled on a purple paisley skirt and slipped on a pair of flip-flops. The oversized gray T-shirt she slept in bunched around her waist. Grabbing her purse and her keys, she headed for the door.

Cheryl was so tired that she didn't know how she managed to drive to Adam's condo, but she got there somehow. Propelled by frustration, she jumped out of the car and went into the building, bursting through the glass doors like an action hero. By the time she got to his door, her fatigue had faded away.

Thump, thump, thump. She beat the door, determined to wake him. She waited a few seconds before knocking again.

"Who is it?" Adam said through the door.

"It's me, Cheryl. Open up." He had tried on several occasions to give her the key to his place, but she always refused to take it. Even if she had a key, she wouldn't just walk in, in the middle of the night.

She heard the click of the lock, and the door swung open. He had obviously already been awake. He still wore the clothes he was wearing earlier. "What's wrong?"

"Can I come in?" Her frustration dissipated when she saw his face.

"Of course." He stepped to the side so she could come in, then pulled the door closed behind her. "What's wrong?"

As soon as she walked into his apartment, the music in her head stopped. Relief washed over her. This was all she had wanted. "The music has been going nonstop in my head." She dropped her purse on the sofa. "I can't sleep. I can't do anything."

He ran his fingers through his dark hair. "That sucks. I

only just finished going through the videos from Stephanie's." He opened his mouth like he was going to say something else but changed his mind. "You must be exhausted. Can you hear the music now?"

Cheryl shook her head. "It's the first peace I've had in hours." She couldn't hold back a yawn. "Anything else interesting on the videos?"

"As a matter of fact, there is." He walked over to the bar and picked up his tablet. "Take a look at this." He handed it to her.

Cheryl pressed play and watch the grainy black and white footage. It played at a plodding speed. On it, the girl that she had seen in Stephanie and Will's house skipped across the screen. She wore the same party dress she had on when Cheryl saw her. "That's her! That's the girl we saw." When she pointed at the screen, she touched it, pausing the video. She hadn't intended to do that, but she held the tablet up and looked at the image of the girl's profile caught in mid-movement.

"I thought so." Adam stood next to her, looking at the screen. "Who is she?" He reached over and touched the screen, so the video began to play again.

The girl skipped across the living room before vanishing at the glass doors. Cheryl ran the video back and watched it again. "What does she want?" Her eyelids drooped as she looked at the screen. She needed to lie down now and get some sleep. She yawned so wide she could feel the corners of her mouth stretching. "Can I sleep here tonight? I'm so tired I can't function. We can go over all this in the morning."

He put his tablet down on the bar and stretched his arms over his head. "You're always welcome here. I'm exhausted too."

She couldn't wait to lie down and finally get some rest. She knew that they had a lot to figure out in the morning.

**

Cheryl lay curled into Adam. The ends of her dark hair tickled his nose. He turned his head away from her. She slept heavily beside him. Before she'd drifted off to sleep, she told him that she felt like she hadn't slept in days. He knew the feeling because he hadn't slept either, and tonight was no different. He lay on his back, looking at the ceiling. He'd given up on closing his eyes, trying to force himself into sleep because it was bringing him more frustration than rest.

He tried to guess the time, maybe four-thirty in the morning. He couldn't be sure. He wasn't going to look at his phone to find out.

Cheryl snored softly beside him. An uncomfortable heat radiated from her body. He rolled over so his back faced her and pushed the sheets off of him. Adam had blackout shades in his room. He had installed them recently when he realized that the streetlamps outside were ruining his sleep. He'd enjoyed the total darkness of the room while he slept, but tonight he realized that one of the shades was not pulled all the way down. There was a crack of about a half an inch that let in a narrow column of light. Because it was the only thing he could see in the darkness, he focused on that and listened to the sound of Cheryl sleeping. Then he swore he saw something moving in the darkness. A shadow flashed across the room, only becoming visible for a few seconds in the narrow beam of light. Adam froze. "Did you see that?" he whispered, knowing full well that Cheryl was asleep.

She answered with a grunt before the rhythm of her breathing returned to normal. She rolled over.

He saw it again. It flashed by the strip of light. He listened, straining his ears but heard nothing. He had just decided to get up to investigate when he felt the hot breath on his face. Hot and damp, it smelled like rot. Adam's instinct was to lie perfectly still, hoping that if he didn't move, it wouldn't realize he was there. In reality, it was too late to use such a technique because he had already spoken. He held his breath. His heart thumping in his chest, he waited. The hot air moved across his face. It went down the length of his body to the toes of his right foot hanging off the edge of the bed. His heart beat faster still as he imagined a giant mouth full of sharp teeth encircling his foot. Was he feeling something, or was it all his imagination?

He couldn't lay frozen. He needed to protect Cheryl from whatever it was. He gathered all his courage and sat up. "Get out of here!" he yelled as he reached for his cell phone. He touched the screen, hoping that turning it on would provide enough light to help him see what it was. That was not the case. The phone only let off a slight glow. So he leaped to his feet and, rushing over to the window, pushed up the blind, revealing nothing.

Cheryl let out a tiny yelp. She sat up, holding the sheet up over her chest. "What's wrong?"

Adam turned on the light. A soft yellow glow pushed into the darkness. "Nothing," he said. "I thought something was in here with us."

She immediately got out of bed, wrapping the sheet around herself, and walked around the room. She even stooped down, looking beneath the bed. "I don't see anything, but that doesn't mean there wasn't anything here."

"I know."

They sat on the edge of the bed together. She leaned her head on his shoulder and let out a satisfying yawn.

"What do you think it was?" Her voice was soft and slow

like she was on the edges of drifting off to sleep again.

"I don't know. I didn't see anything, but I swear I felt its breath on me." Even though he hadn't seen anything, the image that formed in his mind was that of a large hairy monster with sharp, fang-like teeth. He wouldn't dare say that to Cheryl because it wasn't based on anything.

"If you felt breath, it wasn't a ghost." She was right, and the idea sent chills through him.

Cheryl was oddly undisturbed by what had just happened. She crawled back into bed, and before he knew it, she was sleeping again. After what he had just experienced, Adam couldn't sleep. His mind was working too hard. His senses were searching the darkness, waiting for whatever it was to return.

Chapter 12

"Stephanie's gone." Will didn't even wait for Cheryl to say hello before he started speaking. "I've been looking all over, and she isn't here." This was the first time Cheryl had ever heard him sound like he didn't have control over the situation.

"When was the last time you saw her?" Cheryl was sitting at Adam's kitchen table, drinking a cup of coffee, waiting for him to get out of the shower.

"Last night." The panic in his voice unnerved her. "We went to bed at the same time. Then when I woke up, she was gone. There was dirt all over the floor, and the sliding glass door in the living room was open."

"Did you check with your neighbors to see if they saw anything?" Cheryl got up from the table and went to the bathroom. She put her hand over the receiver and yelled in. "Stephanie's disappeared!"

Adam said something, but she couldn't hear him.

"I went knocking on doors, but only one person answered, and he didn't see anything. I called her friends, and no one's heard from her. Her cell phone is here." Cheryl could picture him holding up Stephanie's phone with the sparky rose gold cover.

"You didn't notice anything in the middle of the night. You didn't hear any strange noises or notice when she got out of bed." She hoped that guiding him through some possibilities might trigger a memory.

"No. Nothing." He paused. "When I called for her, and she didn't answer, I thought maybe she was outside. She doesn't like going in the backyard, but she has been sleepwalking occasionally, and I'd found her back there before. Then when I saw the doors open, I thought that must be where she was, but she wasn't."

"We haven't had time to do much research, but we'll head back up to see you. Did you check the videos at all?" She knew Adam didn't like people messing with the cameras but felt like this was an unusual circumstance.

"No."

"Go ahead and look at the videos. We'll be there soon."

Adam came out of the bathroom, drying himself off.

"Get dressed," Cheryl said. "We have to go back to Sarasota."   She   called   Day.

**

Day didn't have anyone to cover her shop, so she stayed there to work on research while Cheryl and Adam went to Sarasota to find out what had happened to Stephanie.

Will seemed to have aged overnight. The creases in his forehead had deepened, and dark circles ringed his eyes.

"What time did you realize Stephanie was missing?" Adam asked.

Will looked at the ground. His upper lip twitched. "I didn't notice until I woke up this morning around six." He lifted his gaze to Adam's face. "What if she's out wandering in the woods alone? Terrible things happen in those woods." He wrung his hands.

"What kind of terrible things?" Adam asked, wondering

if he knew something about the nature preserve that he hadn't bothered to share with them.

"You never know what people might do when they think no one is watching." Will's voice was flat.

Adam wasn't sure why he felt the need to explore this subject even further. "Like what?"

Will scowled. "People do all sorts of terrible things. I don't even want to imagine." Will looked at the floor and shook his head. After a few moments, he turned his back to them and went into the house. "Come in," he said as he shuffled into the living room. Dark dirt lay scattered across the white tile floors. "It was like this when I woke up. I left it in case it would help you figure out what happened." He stepped over the piles of dirt, careful not to mess them up any more than they already were.

"Did you see anything on any of the videos?" Cheryl asked.

Adam hadn't realized she had told him he could watch the videos without them. He hated the idea of it, mostly because he didn't like Will very much. He could've erased footage he didn't want them to see. How could they trust that anything on them was authentic now?

"Yes. She's on all of them." Will picked up a camera. He had removed all of them from their tripods and placed them on the bar. He flipped through the screens before handing one to Cheryl. "She's on this one, looking just like she did on the video from the other night."

Adam stood next to Cheryl so they could watch the video together. It was very much reminiscent of the one from the night before. Stephanie walked up the hallway. This time she looked at the ground, walking on her tiptoes.

"She's in all of them." Will walked over to them, holding another camera. "On this one, you can see that she goes outside and then vanishes. It looks like she walks right through the fence." He looked at the sliding glass doors. "We should look for her in the woods."

"Is this the camera that was looking out into the yard?" Cheryl asked.

"Yeah, I think so." He handed it to her and then walked over to the sliding glass doors, pushed them open, and stepped outside.

Cheryl and Adam watched the video. In it, Stephanie dressed only in a nightgown, stepped out into the yard, and walked right up to the fence, but what Will had described was not exactly what happened. He had missed something, but Adam saw it now. A round hole opened up in the fence just like the one he had seen open up in the living room wall. Inside it, the forest teemed with life. Stephanie stepped through the hole. She didn't hesitate. She didn't look back.

"Did you see that?" he asked Cheryl when the video was over. "Did you see the hole?"

Cheryl nodded. "I don't think we're going to find her in the nature preserve."

**

Stephanie had walked into a different world, but she hadn't realized it until her opportunity to leave had sealed up behind her. When she came to her senses, she found herself standing in the middle of a dense forest. Beneath the light of a full, silvery moon, she saw large smooth oval leaves jutting out from prehistoric-looking plants. Giant trees towered over her head; their twisted branches swayed in the wind.

Stephanie turned around, expecting to see the fence that separated her backyard from the forest, but the fence was no longer there. It had disappeared. In its place stood a cluster of trees and undergrowth.

She turned around in a full circle, searching for something that looked familiar. She hadn't yet realized the peril she was in, and yet tears were already welling up in her eyes. "Will!" She called out to him, even though she knew she was probably too far away for him to hear her. Wherever she was, it was far away from home. Could she have walked that far in her sleep? Had she been sleepwalking at all? She remembered feeling like she was in a trance. She remembered getting up and walking down the hallway, mesmerized by the trail of dirt. Something had grabbed hold of her soul, forcing her to pull the door open and step outside. Even though she might have appeared to have done it all of her own free will, she had not. There was something intangible nudging her forward. Too bad she couldn't explain exactly what that was. She remembered going out into the yard, but after that, she couldn't recall anything. Had she walked around the side of the house? Had she opened the side gate and walked into the midst of the neighborhood in only her pajamas? Had she wandered into the woods? She looked down at her white nightgown that reached her knees. Her feet were bare, and the earth beneath them was cool and damp.

Life surrounded her. She heard it scurrying beneath the leaves and singing out rhythmically from the trees. The animals hid in the cover of darkness, but they were unafraid of being heard.

"Will!" Calling him was useless. She knew that, but there was no one else to call. "Help!" Maybe that would get someone's attention. "Help!"

She listened, hoping to hear a human voice respond to her call. The only response was the chirping of crickets and the croaking of frogs. The feeling of dread she often felt in the backyard came to her now. It crept up her like a spider crawling up her leg. Her breath quickened, and terror shot through her. She turned and, without considering what direction she was going, began to run. For all she knew, she was running into the very danger she was trying to avoid. As long as she was running, she felt like she was doing something to keep herself safe. Branches snagged her nightgown and scratched her shins as she went. She panted, pumping her legs as quickly as they would go. Sharp objects drove into the soles of her feet, but she ignored the pain and continued onward, fearful that if she stopped, she would lose her life. She had covered a good distance before she slipped on wet leaves and fell into the dirt, twisting her ankle. She yelped with pain. She couldn't afford to lay still. She scrambled to her feet, but as she went to move, she felt something grabbing hold of her ankle. She jerked her foot forward, trying to run but stumbled again. She clawed at the ground, trying desperately to get to her feet, but she couldn't. She looked down to see dark vines wrapped around her ankles, reaching up her calves. Yelling, she reached down, pulling at them, but they were wrapped tightly and would not come loose.

"No!"

It didn't take long for her protest to turn to incomprehensible sobs and squeals. The vines slithered up from the forest floor, winding themselves around her legs, gripping them tightly, but the more she struggled, the tighter they grabbed hold. She kicked her legs in a panic and pulled at tree roots and trunks in a desperate attempt to get away.

"Help! Please, someone help me!" She would not give up. If she had to, she would fight to the bitter end. As she squirmed and wriggled, the vines moved up her legs, wrapping themselves tightly around her hips and her waist. They continued to move up her, and she wondered if they would squeeze her to death, much like a boa constrictor kills its prey. Just then, she saw movement in the darkness among the trees. Was it an animal, coming to finish off what the vines had started? She didn't know whether to call out for help again or to remain silent, hoping not to be discovered. She watched. Her brain raced. Quietly she yanked at the vines as she watched the movement in the trees. Then she realized that if she could see whatever it was, it could probably see her. Her silence didn't matter because they were looking at her now, and she could make out their forms in among the shadows. It was two people, one a tall adult and the other was the girl in the red dress. A group of small animals gathered at their feet, running circles around their legs as they walked forward. She'd seen this before in a dream and knew what to expect. The woman held the child's hand. A large opossum sat perched on the woman's shoulders, its pink tail curling around her neck. "Help me!" she pleaded.

The girl looked up at the woman as if asking for permission to act. The woman shook her head. They walked together hand in hand, taking their time as they approached Stephanie. They acted as if they had all the time in the world, while Stephanie felt like her life was slipping away. The vines coiled around her body. She could already feel her feet and calves growing numb. She writhed around on the ground, desperate to break free. "Please! Help me!"

The woman angled her face at Stephanie. Roaches, crickets, and grasshoppers pulsated as they crawled across each other on her face. Her skin was a wave of movement.

The sight of her sent Stephanie into a panic. She let out a guttural scream and pushed at the vines around her waist, trying to push them off.

"I didn't do anything wrong. All my life, I've tried to do what's right. Sure I've made some mistakes but--" The vines tightened their grip. "What's happening? Why is this happening to me?" She wailed.

The little girl looked at her with wide, concerned eyes. She held her finger to her lips as if telling Stephanie to be quiet.

Stephanie ignored her and continued to howl with fear.

The girl gripped the woman's hand tighter and looked around them. She was frightened. Something was coming. The woman reached out her hand, crawling with insects, toward Stephanie's face. Stephanie tried to recoil, but the vines held her still. "Don't touch me!"

Those were the last words she remembered uttering.

Chapter 13

Adam stepped into the backyard. Will stood in front of the fence at the exact spot where Stephanie had walked through the now nonexistent hole.

"She was right here, and then she was gone." He reached out and touched the graying planks of wood. "You saw it."

"I did, but I also saw something that you didn't. Stephanie didn't just disappear; she stepped into another dimension." Adam wasn't sure how to describe this to someone who couldn't see it for himself.

Will jerked his head around to look at Adam, twisting his face at him.

"I know it's hard to believe, but I saw it when I was in your house before. Right above the couch, a hole opened up into another world." The look in Will's eyes made him feel foolish.

Cheryl came outside, holding one of the cameras in her hand. "What's going on out here?"

Will was still looking at Adam. "So you're trying to tell me that Stephanie is in a different dimension right now?" He waved his arms around in front of his face when he said "different dimension" like he was imitating a comical magician.

"What's more believable, that or that she just disappear?" Adam scowled. "You can go out in the woods to search for her as much as you want, but you won't find her. She's not there."

"He's right," Cheryl said. "She's in a parallel world."

"What do you mean... parallel world?" He raised his voice and gestured toward the fence.

"Whether you believe it or not, it's true." Adam noticed the tingling feeling in his fingertips. The sense of dread he had experienced in the yard before was returning. "Do you feel that?" he asked Cheryl.

Cheryl swallowed. Adam hadn't really looked at her before, but now he saw the distant look in her eyes. She nodded before pointing at the fence. "They're coming."

Adam turned and looked at the fence. He saw a spot the size of a quarter where the wood seemed to have turned to liquid. The hole was opening up again.

**

"Who's coming?" Will asked. He looked at the fence where Cheryl was pointing.

Cheryl wanted to run back into the house through the living room out the front door and get back in Adam's car to speed away. Her job was to stay. She owed that much to Stephanie.

A small section of the fence seemed to turn to liquid. It undulated and shone in the sunlight.

Will double over, his arms grasping his waist as he fell to his knees and began to vomit in the grass. Thick black liquid poured from his mouth.

Cheryl's insides turned, but she took a deep breath and focused on the soles of her feet, connecting her to the earth to prevent herself from retching. She needed to stay focused to see what happened next. She hoped more than anything that the hole would open up again, and Stephanie would step out uninjured and unaffected by the experience.

Will was on his hands and knees now. He had stopped throwing up, but his breathing was shallow and raspy.

"Maybe you should go inside." She stepped forward and put her hand on his back, trying not to look at the black vomit beneath him.

He swallowed and gazed up at her with sweat streaming down his face.

Adam walked over and took his arm. "Come on. This is too much for you. Go inside. We'll deal with it."

Adam helped Will inside, but Cheryl was only vaguely aware of what was happening now. The fence held her focus. She stepped closer. The desire to touch the dark moving spot welled up in her. She wondered what would happen if she did. Would it swallow her hand? Would it suck her into another plane of existence?

She was standing about a foot from the opening now. It had not materialized into a hole just yet. She raised her hand in front of her, reaching out a finger to touch it. A high pitch ring sounded in her ears as she moved her fingertip closer and closer. The way it moved mesmerized her. It seemed to pull her hand toward it, but just before she made contact, Adam yanked her away.

"What are you doing?" He grabbed her shoulders and pulled her back. "Don't get too close. You don't know what will happen."

"I just wanted to touch it."

"That's a bad idea," he said with such authority that it made her want to rebel.

"I know, but--" Something about it seemed so inviting. Now that he'd broken her out of the trance it had lulled her into, that familiar sense of dread returned. She swallowed, hoping to push the acrid taste rising in her throat back down. The fence returned to normal.

"Are you okay?" His face was so close to hers.

"Yeah," she said, but she was shaking her head no. "I need to go inside."

He took hold of her hand and led her inside, where Will sat on the sofa with his head in his hands.

"Are you hanging in there?" Adam asked. He led Cheryl over to the chair at the far end of the room. It was good to sit down in it for a little while. She wouldn't be able to rest long. They needed to find Stephanie.

Adam sat down on the sofa next to Will. His complexion had grown sallow. He closed his eyes for a few seconds.

She sat back in the soft lounge chair and concentrated all her efforts on not throwing up. Since everyone else's eyes were closed, she closed hers too. Soon her churning stomach settled, and her muscles relaxed. She blinked her eyes open. She knew she had only been sitting there for a few minutes, but it felt like she had drifted off for hours.

It took a moment for the room around her to come into focus. Adam and Will still sat on the couch with their eyes closed to the world. She watched the men, sitting side by side, heavy with exhaustion.

Cheryl noticed movement in her peripheral vision. She turned her head only slightly to look out the glass sliding doors. The bug woman was out there. She stood at the glass, looking in with vacant holes that should have been her eyes. Her flesh crawled with masses of insects. Cheryl was immediately repulsed.

"She's here again." Cheryl got up. Her repulsion could not stand in the way of her knowing the truth. Whatever this woman was, she might know what happened to Stephanie. She had to talk to her.

Adam's eyes snapped open. "Who?"

"Stephanie?" Will hopped up off of the sofa.

"No, not Stephanie." Cheryl rushed to the glass door. Overriding her instincts to run from this woman, she approached her. "Your ghost."

Adam was up now, walking next to her. He looked through the sliding glass doors with an unmistakable look of fear on his face, and Cheryl knew he saw her too. "What are you doing?" He spoke in a low whisper.

Cheryl whispered back even though she didn't know why they were whispering. "I have to talk to her."

"Talk to who?" Will looked around the room before returning his gaze to the glass doors. "I don't see anyone."

"You can't see her, but that doesn't mean she's not there." Cheryl was at the door now. The woman had moved. She stood so close to the glass that the ants and termites that made up her nose squirmed only about an inch from it. Cheryl gulped down her fear as she reached for the handle. She looked at Adam and said, "Here goes nothing."

The door glided open. Cheryl and the woman stood face-to-face. Cheryl swallowed with a gulp. The woman didn't move. The opossum perched on her shoulder lifted its head. Its pointed pink nose twitched as it sniffed her. The animals circling the woman's feet all froze. Cheryl reached out her hand slowly and grabbed hold of Adam's arm for reassurance.

"Don't move," she said to him. She took a deep breath, and the rich scent of freshly tilled soil filled her lungs. She exhaled slowly, trying to calm her thumping heart.

The woman tilted her head, and a giant cockroach fell to the ground and skittered away. The opossum flicked its tail.

"Where is Stephanie?" Cheryl spoke precisely.

She swore the woman would answer. She saw a spark of something in the opossum's eyes. The woman opened her mouth. Before she could say anything, Will came rushing up behind them. "This is crazy!" he yelled. "My fiancée is missing, and you're talking to nothing in my backyard. Do you think the trees are going to tell you where she is?" Startled, Cheryl turned to look at him.

"Calm down. The ghost is here." Adam reached out to put his hand on his shoulder, but Will knocked it away.

"This is crazy! I told Stephanie I didn't want you guys here doing this. Now she's missing because she believed you. I should've never called you!"

Cheryl turned away from them back to the woman who she half expected to be gone.

"I'm Cheryl. Who are you? What are you doing here?" She found that sometimes no matter how strange a ghost might seem, talking to them like they were one of the living worked.

The opossum lunged forward, bearing a mouthful of pointed teeth. Cheryl stumbled back, falling onto the floor.

A chorus of snarls and growls met her. The squirrels and raccoons reared up on their back legs, baring their teeth. Cheryl screeched with fear. Adam rushed over to her just as the thousands of insects that made up the woman's body collapsed into a skittering pile on the ground and ran away, squeezing through the cracks in the back fence. The animals vanished. In their place, where the woman had been standing, something white laid on the patio. Cheryl crawled her hands and knees toward it.

"What's that?" She heard Will ask behind her.

"I don't know." Reluctantly she reached out, taking the white fabric between her thumb and forefinger and lifting it from the ground. "It looks like some kind of dress." It was a simple white sleeveless frock with lace trim around the hem.

"That's Stephanie's nightgown. That's what

she was wearing when she disappeared." Will's voice cracked with emotion. Cheryl sat on the sofa in Stephanie and Will's living room, watching as Will talked to a short detective with a mustache that reminded Cheryl of a 1970s private eye. The detective focused all of his attention on Adam and Will and didn't seem interested in talking to Cheryl. So, she sat back, dreamily watching them for a few minutes before she realized that she didn't have to. Stephanie may have stepped into a parallel dimension, but she knew that dimension was connected to the wilderness behind their house. If she went there, maybe she could find Stephanie. Nothing was stopping her from getting up and starting her search right then. As the three men talked in the living room, she eased off the sofa and went to the front door. She was certain one of them would notice her slipping away. As she pulled the door open, she waited to hear Adam call her name, but when he didn't she stepped outside and softly pulled the door closed behind her.

"Are you sure?" Adam asked.

"How did it get there? It was like it just materialized from thin air." Will reached down and snatched the nightgown from Cheryl's trembling hands. He held it up in front of him by the shoulders so they could get a better look at it. It was streaked with dirt. A long tear ran down the side seam. In the center, about where Stephanie's stomach would be if she were wearing it, was a bloodstain the size of a grapefruit.

Will threw the nightgown onto the couch. "That's it. I'm calling the police."

Chapter 14

The wind pushed against her, whipping through her hair and wrapping her skirt tight against her legs. Soft, white clouds raced across the sky. She stood on the front porch and looked out across the thick, green lawn in need of mowing.

Stephanie and Will's house sat in a cul-de-sac where a sliver of land dense with trees led into the nature preserve. She walked down to the end of the driveway, past the police car and up the quiet road. There were no sidewalks in this neighborhood, forcing her to walk in the street. She only had to pass three houses before she got to the path that snaked its way through a cluster of trees into the nature preserve. Two large oaks stood at the head of the path, their thick trunks extended skyward. Silvery Spanish moss hung from the crooks of their gnarled branches. Cheryl turned back to look at Stephanie and Will's small Mediterranean house to see if anyone had come outside yet looking for her. The porch was empty. The red front door was shut tight.

She had her cell phone with her, so Adam could call when he   noticed   she   was   missing.

**

Will shifted his weight back and forth as he talked to the

detective. He pulled his hands from his pockets and shoved them back in again about a dozen times. His gaze bounced all around the room, never quite landing on anyone.

Adam wondered what he was doing. If he didn't calm down, the detective would think he was guilty of something.

"So you look for ghosts?" The detective smirked.

Adam understood. He was used to this by now, but that didn't mean he didn't tire of it. "Yeah," he said. "Anyway, we set up cameras. These were the last videos of Stephanie before she disappeared." He played the video to the detective, who seemed interested.

"Does she have a history of sleepwalking?" he asked while still looking at the video.

"Not before we moved here." Will watched the video too. "A lot of weird things have been happening since we moved in. That's why Stephanie wanted to hire--" He pointed at Adam.

The detective let out a dry laugh before opening his mouth to say something and then changing his mind. "Has she left the house when she was sleepwalking before?"

"Once I found her in the backyard. That only happened that one time though." Will frowned.

Adam wondered what he was thinking.

"She could've been sleepwalking, and some whack job saw her and--" The detective stopped and looked at Will before handing him the camera.

Adam considered showing him the final video. He wondered if Will would mention it. He waited, watching them. When Will said nothing, he decided he had better. The best way to make sure this was a thorough police investigation was to make sure the police had all the information. Whether or not they would believe it was another story. "You should see this too." Adam brought the camera that had recorded the backyard over to the policeman.

He watched it in silence. When Stephanie disappeared at the end, he looked over at Adam and said, "Looks like there's a glitch in your video."

"I don't think so." Adam looked him in the eye.

"Of course, you don't." He handed the camera back to Adam. "So, from this video, we can see that she went outside. I'm betting she went out the gate and around into the neighborhood. I'll talk to the neighbors and see if any of them were up late last night and saw something. The good thing here is that we have a timestamp."

"They were probably all asleep." Will hunched his shoulders

"They probably were, but it's worth asking." The detective headed for the front door.

Adam turned and noticed Cheryl was no longer sitting in the living room. "Cheryl!" He walked down the hallway.

"She went outside about thirty minutes ago." The detective opened the door and stepped outside.

Adam followed. Standing on the front porch, he scanned the area, hoping to see her. When he didn't, he immediately pulled his phone from his pocket and called her number. It went directly to voicemail. "Come on, Cheryl. Why don't you have your phone on?"

"She's not answering?" Will asked.

"No. I'm going to wander around and look for her." Adam walked down the driveway to the street.

"She probably went into the woods to look for Stephanie." Will pointed up the street. "We can get in over there."

Adam did his best to be optimistic. He found in life that things worked out for him most of the time, but he didn't have a good feeling about this. Cheryl's abilities made her particularly vulnerable during their investigations. It wasn't uncommon for her to end up in trouble.

As they approached the path that led into the woods, they saw the detective talking to one of the neighbors, a rail-thin man who looked to be in his late seventies, leaning on a wooden cane.

"We're going to look for her in the woods," Will called to the detective, who nodded at them in response. "Don't do anything stupid," he said as they passed.

Ancient-looking oak trees flanked the entrance to the nature preserve. The path itself was sandy and easy to walk. As they stepped into the preserve, the dense canopy overhead blocked out the intense sunlight. The tangle of vegetation on either side of them would make veering off the path difficult. They were only a couple yards into the preserve when they came to a fork in the path. "We should go that way," Adam said, pointing to the right. "That should take us close to the area behind your house. If she walked through that hole in your fence--"

"What hole?" Will hurried up the path in the direction Adam had suggested.

"Nothing." Adam walked behind him, scanning the dense underbrush on either side of the path, looking for signs that someone had ventured off the assigned route into the woods. Branches bowed and swayed in the wind. Geckos crossed in front of them. When they came across a black racer snake lying in the sand, it raised its head and smelled them with its forked tongue before slithering into the foliage. Adam listened as they walked. The squeaks, squawks, and chirps were familiar, belonging to birds and squirrels. He knew there must be more than that living among the trees. He had seen so much more in his visions.

Dread wrapped around Adam. This was supposed to be a simple haunting case, but the state of Stephanie's nightgown suggested that it had turned into much more. After the Ridge Point case, he'd hoped they'd put murder investigations behind   them.

**

Cheryl followed the path as it hooked around behind the neighborhood houses. The further she walked, the thicker the vegetation around her became. Branches reached out toward her. tangling in her curly hair, snagging her skirt. The animals in the forest though hidden from sight, weren't shy. Their calls drifted through the air. Even though civilization was not far away, Cheryl heard no cars, air-conditioning units, or airplanes passing overhead. She was alone in the wilderness. The wind picked up, and the trees danced, their great branches swaying overhead.

The dread that Cheryl felt in Stephanie and Will's backyard continued. As she moved forward on the path, it intensified. Adrenaline pumped through her as she forced herself forward, ignoring her instincts to spin around on her heels and leave the way she came. Stephanie was her best friend. She had been her friend when no one else was. Cheryl refused to let fear keep her from helping her. To do that would be unforgivable. She knew that if she were in a similar situation, Stephanie would do everything she could to help her too.

Cheryl thought she was walking parallel to the row of houses on the street. Her sense of direction had never been great, but she had made a series of rights to get to where she was, and by her calculations, the houses should have been on her right side.

When the dread got so intense that she thought she might not be able to take it anymore, she stopped on the sandy path. Patches of dark grass grew in the white sand. She bent over, putting her hands on her knees. The front of her long teal skirt hung to the ground. Her stomach churned, and bile rose in her throat. This must be where their house is, she thought. She swallowed hard, pushing down the terrible feeling. She closed her eyes, and the world spun around her. What if she fell over in the wilderness and got dragged off by a panther? She needed to keep going. As she straightened up, another wave of nausea came over her. The croaking and screeching and squawking grew. The noise was so loud that she covered her ears with her hands. She fell to her knees. The high-pitched noises burrowed into her. She opened her eyes and looked around her only to see the trees swaying even quicker.

"Stop it! Stop it!" She yelled at the sounds. As if obeying her, they stopped. Cheryl removed her hands from her ears, and it was truly silent. The trees continued to sway in the breeze. Geckos puffed out the throats. Cheryl heard nothing. The world around her was empty and silent. She knelt in the dirt. Tiny pebbles pressed into the skin of her knees through her thin skirt. She cleared her throat, and it turned into a cough. One cough turned into another, and another until she felt something sharp and solid in her mouth. She gagged and coughed and spat onto the ground. A giant roach about three inches in length hit the white sand and scurried away. Its brown body glistened with saliva. Upon seen it, Cheryl was so busy gagging that she didn't notice that her hearing had come back. The screeches and caws from the forest erupted again at an even greater volume.

Cheryl spat into the dirt in front of her, desperate to get any hint of the insect out of her mouth but swore she still felt the prickly sensation of its feet on her tongue. She heaved, but nothing came out of her--no vomit and fortunately, no more insects.

Panic flooded over her, and she hopped to her feet.

"Stephanie!" She called with no evidence that Stephanie was even near. She looked down at the ground to see the path had vanished. Bushes and vines surrounded her. She stood in a tiny patch of bare ground, only two feet across in either direction. The forest around her became so disorienting that she had no idea which way to go to get back into the neighborhood.

"Help!" she called. Maybe Adam and Will had come back into the woods, looking for her or looking for Stephanie. She cupped her hands around her mouth to amplify the sound of her voice and called out again. The screeching from the forest died back, leaving space for other ambient noises to push through--rustling leaves in the trees and the rushing of wind. Leaves crunched beneath someone or something's feet. Something was approaching her. She spun in a circle, looking into the trees hoping to see whatever was headed her way before it got to her.

When she spotted it in the brush, she nearly laughed. A scruffy-haired opossum, the size of a large house cat, ambled toward her. It wasn't moving quickly, but Cheryl remembered how the opossum that sat on the ghost woman's shoulders had bared its teeth at her earlier. While she was confident she could outrun it, she was curious about its approach.

A twig snapped behind her. Spinning around, she found herself once again face-to-face with the bug woman. Palmetto bugs scurried back and forth across the woman's forehead. Cheryl gulped down the lump in her throat.

"What have you done to Stephanie?" Cheryl watched the woman's face as the bugs writhed across it. The coal-black spaces where her eyes should've been seemed to suck in all the light around her. "Where is she?"

The corners of the woman's lips pulled up into a slight smile. She bent down, and Cheryl jumped back, afraid that she was reaching out to grab her. Instead, she placed her hand on the ground, and the opossum climbed up her arm to return to its normal resting place on her shoulders. It wrapped its pink tail around her neck as it settled. When the woman stood, the opossum's pointed face was close to Cheryl's shoulder. Remembering the sharpness of its teeth, she took a step back. It looked at her with black eyes and twitched its pink nose before opening its mouth. "You'll see soon," it said with a voice so deep it vibrated the wall of Cheryl's chest.

She put her hand over her heart and took another step back. "You speak?"

Neither the woman nor the opossum showed any interest in her question. The woman turned around and sauntered back into the trees. The opossum clambered around on her shoulders, turning its face to watch Cheryl. Its beady eyes remained on her until both the opossum and the woman disappeared among the trees.

"Cheryl!" Adam's voice cracked her sense of fear. He had come for her. When she looked all around, she was standing on the path again. No shrubbery or underbrush blocked her way. She turned, facing the direction his voice came from, and saw him and Will in the distance. As soon as she came into view, Adam began running. Cheryl was so excited to see him again that she ran too. When they reached each other, they embraced. She held on to him like she hadn't seen him in years.

Even though it'd only been a few hours at most, it felt like she was never going to get out of the woods again. She was so relieved that, for a moment, she'd forgotten all about Stephanie and why she was out there in the first place.

It wasn't until Will didn't turn around to head back toward the house that she remembered. As they hugged in the middle of the path, he had pushed past them continuing forward.

"You haven't seen any hint of her?" he asked.

Cheryl broke her embrace with Adam. "No, but I saw your ghost again."

Will turned around. "It's not my ghost." He walked backward on the path for a few steps before spinning back around and continuing forward at a fast and steady clip.

"The woman or the girl?" Adam asked. He had started walking again, following Will.

She took a few fast steps to catch up with him and then grabbed hold of his hand. "The bug woman. This time the opossum talked to me."

"Are you all right?" Will looked back at them over his shoulder. He moved swiftly up the path, ducking tree limbs and hopping over trees that had fallen across the path. "You didn't fall and hit your head or anything, did you?"

Cheryl had thought she was speaking quietly enough for him not to hear. "I'm fine... Now."

"Okay, then." Cheryl hated the sarcasm in his voice.

"What did he say to you?" Adam asked.

"You believe her?" Will slowed a bit, looking back at Adam, surprised.

Cheryl wondered if Will realized that they had gone too far. She suspected they had because the dreadful feeling she got around the house began to lessen.

"Of course, I believe her." He turned back and winked at her, lightening the mood.

If the situation had been even slightly different, Cheryl probably would've laughed. She scanned the trees as they passed and looked in the underbrush for evidence that someone had gone off the path. If Stephanie had passed through here, she definitely wouldn't have confined her wanderings to the path. "He didn't say much, just that I'd see."

"See what?" Adam asked.

"I don't know." Just then, a flash of white amongst the deep green of the forest caught her eye. "I see something." She stopped and pointed.

Adam and Will stopped too. "Me too." Adam went bounding into the forest, trudging through the underbrush. Cheryl wouldn't have done that, afraid of what might have been hiding out of sight. He untangled the strip of white fabric from a bush. When he got it loose, he held it up.

"What?" Too impatient to wait for him to come back to the path, Will went into the forest to meet him.

Cheryl stayed put, watching them from the safety of the path. She didn't have to get a closer look to know what it was. It was obvious to her. Stephanie had been here. They were getting close.

Chapter 15

As soon as he saw the strip of white fabric, he knew it was Stephanie's. They were on the right track. He untangled it from the thorny vine and held it up. Unlike Stephanie's torn nightgown, this piece of fabric was completely white and clean.

"That's from her nightgown." Will ran over and took the fabric from him. "She must be around here somewhere." He looked at the ground as if looking for footprints. Then he ran off into the woods yelling, "Stephanie! Stephanie!"

Adam looked over at Cheryl, who stood on the path, watching them.

"Maybe we should spread out and look for her." Adam was surprised that Cheryl would suggest such a thing, but he had also been surprised that she had wandered back into the woods alone.

"Turn your phone on so we can contact each other." He turned and looked in the direction Will had run off in. He was already so far back in the woods that he was nearly out of sight.

Cheryl reached into the pocket of her skirt and pulled out her phone. "You're right. It's off. Sorry, I didn't realize it before I left."

"I know. I tried to call you when I noticed you were gone.

I was worried sick." He had never been a worrier before, but Cheryl made him that way.

She looked down at her phone suddenly. "Day's calling."

"Answer it." He stepped closer so he could hear their conversation. Cheryl didn't put it on speaker, so he listened to her side of the conversation.

"What's going on? What's she saying?" He leaned in closer, so his ear nearly touched the phone.

"Wait a minute," she said into the phone. "Let me tell Adam." She twisted the receiver away from her mouth. "She found a few legends the early settlers used to tell about this area of land being cursed. Explorers would venture out here and never come back."

As if making the realization simultaneously, they both looked out into the forest in the direction Will had gone. "Will!" Adam yelled. He took a few steps into the woods before Cheryl caught hold of his arm.

"A few children have disappeared in the preserve in the last couple of years too."

"The girl?" He looked into the trees hoping to see Will in the distance.

She nodded. "I'm scared." She was holding the phone away from her ear now. Adam could hear Day saying something.

"I have to get Will." The sound of the birds rose in a chorus. Loud and shrill, their calls made it impossible for Adam to think straight. He ran into the woods in the direction he last saw Will. "Will!"

Cheryl ran close behind him. She still held the phone up to her ear. "Just stay on the line in case something happens to us." He heard her say.

They tore through the trees. Cheryl didn't run as fast as Adam wanted her to in her skirt and flip-flops. Neither of them had expected to go hiking through the woods.

"Will! Will, where are you?" They yelled in unison now.

"Slow down. You can't leave me." The birds were so loud now that it was hard for him to hear her, but he stopped and looked behind him. Cheryl stood a few yards away with the phone still pressed to her ear.

"We can't stop. We have to find Will."

She wiped the sweat from her forehead. "I know." She hiked up her skirt and jogged toward him.

Branches cut the skin on his bare legs as he ran. There was no way they would find Will. The area was too large, and he had gotten such a big head start. Adam didn't know how long they were running before he was utterly exhausted. Cheryl had barely managed to keep up. She was quite a ways from him when he finally decided to stop. The light had that golden quality it got just before the sun went down, making the green of the leaves even more vibrant.

"It's getting dark. We might never find our way out of here." Cheryl panted.

"We'll be all right." He looked into the forest where shadows darkened as time ticked by. What would the night bring?

"No, we won't. We've both seen what's out there. They will make sure we aren't all right." She shoved her phone into her pocket. Noticing him looking at it, she said, "My battery ran out." She pulled a hair elastic from her pocket and used it to put her hair into a messy bun. It had gotten frizzy from running around in the woods. "I told her my battery was running out. I should've told her to call the police."

"I still have my phone." He patted it in his pocket.

She looked at him for a moment. "You should try to call Will."

Adam had thought about that already. "I don't have his

number."

She frowned and looked at the ground.

"Don't worry. We'll find our way out. Let's go back that way." He pointed in the direction they had come from. It felt like they'd been running forever. He put his arm around the small of Cheryl's back and guided her through the woods. Mosquitoes buzzed around them. Cheryl waved her hand in front of her face, shooing them away.

"They always bite you more than me," he said. The light changed to blue, and Adam was afraid they really would have to spend the night in the woods.

"That's because I'm sweeter." Cheryl laughed.

Adam figured if they walked long enough, they would find civilization. The nature preserve was not in the middle of nowhere. It was in the center of a suburban neighborhood. Once it got dark, they would easily see lights from passing cars on the street or the illuminated windows of houses. He kept telling himself that as it continued to get darker. The less light, the more life he heard in the trees. There was always something rustling in the branches near his head.

"Did you hear that?" Cheryl stopped and looked around.

"What?" Adam heard so much that he couldn't imagine what one sound she had picked out.

"I thought I heard someone saying something." She stood motionless as if stillness would help her hear better.

"What did it say?" He strained, trying to hear voices beneath all the other sounds of the forest.

"I don't know." She focused.

Adam was keenly aware that they were wasting the little bit of light they had by standing motionless in the forest. "Whatever they're saying, it probably isn't good." He started walking again.

She followed him.

As darkness engulfed them, everything, including the trees, seemed to come alive with motion. The branches reached out for them. The vines crawled toward them, trying to wrap themselves around their ankles.

Adam was mentally preparing himself for a night in the woods when the surroundings started looking familiar. "Wait a minute." This time he was the one who stopped. He didn't have to finish his thought because she had noticed it too.

"We've been here before." She ran ahead of him. "It's the path." She jumped up and down, doing a little victory dance.

"How is that possible? We ran farther than this." Adam turned around and looked back into the woods they'd come from.

"I don't know. Right now, I don't care. All I care about is that we have to go that way"--she pointed--"to get out of here." Only moments ago, he was urging her forward, and now she was practically running up the path. "We're not far from the entrance."

He hurried after her. She was right. They passed through the tall ancient oaks at the entrance of the path in only a few minutes. They stepped out onto the quiet suburban street. Streetlamps lit the way as they walked to Stephanie and Will's house.

"If we found our way out this quickly, maybe Will did too." She said what he had been thinking. They walked up to the front door.

He noticed that all the lights were out. The dark window suggested that Will hadn't found his way out. He rang the doorbell. Then they waited. No one answered.

She slouched. "We've lost them both."

"Don't say that." He reached out and tried the doorknob. It wasn't locked. The door creaked as it eased open, revealing the dark living room.

They looked at each other. Cheryl raised an eyebrow before stepping inside.

He was looking for a light switch when she grabbed hold of his arm, her fingers digging into his flesh. "I think there's someone here."

The hairs on the back of his neck stood on end. There was someone there, and it wasn't Will.

**

Stephanie sat on the floor in the corner, naked and shivering. Bruises and scrapes covered her. Cheryl grabbed a throw from the sofa and draped it around her.

"Oh my goodness, are you okay? We were just looking for you out in the woods. What happened?" Cheryl wanted to say so much more, but she stopped herself.

Stephanie pulled the blanket around herself and looked at the ground. Her teeth chattered. She pushed her back against the wall like she was trying to disappear into the plaster.

"Are you hurt?" Cheryl looked her over for injuries. She turned to tell Adam to call the police, but he was already on the phone.

"We're going to take her to the hospital. Can you meet us there?"

She was already leaving the room when he hung up. "I'll get her some clothes." Something was wrong inside the house. Cheryl couldn't quite put her finger on what, but she felt it. "Does this feel off to you?" She called back down the hall as she approached Will and Stephanie's room. The door was shut tight. She didn't remember the door being closed when they left.

Adam didn't answer.

Cheryl put her hand on the doorknob and then jerked it

away. It was ice cold. She looked up the hall toward the living room and thought about calling for Adam but decided against it. She turned the doorknob and pushed the door open to what should have been Stephanie and Will's bedroom, but when she opened it, a lush jungle greeted her. She snapped the door shut. "Adam!" she called. Something tickled her foot. She looked down to see a giant roach crawl across to big toe. She yelped and kicked her foot out, sending the roach flying through the air.

"What? What's happening?" Adam came running up the hallway.

Cheryl's heart raced, and goosebumps rose on her arms. "Look." She pushed the door open again, revealing a dark bedroom.

"What am I supposed to be seeing?" Adam asked.

"It was just the forest, I swear it." She reached over to the wall and groped for a light switch, flipping it on and washing the room in bright white light.

The little girl in the red dress sat at the end of the bed, clutching her threadbare teddy bear against her chest. "You again." Cheryl charged into the room. Ignoring her fear, she stood in front of the girl. She turned to Adam. "Are you seeing this?"

"Seeing what?"

"The little girl is sitting on the end of the bed." Cheryl wished there was a way for her to know which ghosts Adam would be able to see and which ones he wouldn't.

He shrugged. "I can't see her." He looked down the hallway.

"What's wrong?" Cheryl saw the way he scrunched his face.

"It's just that Stephanie is alone."

"Go check on her." Cheryl was sure not to take her eyes

off the girl.

Adam bounded up the hallway.

"You're not going anywhere this time." She looked the little girl in the eye.

The girl returned a blank stare. She crouched down so she was at eye level with the child, her movements slow and deliberate.

"Who are you?" Cheryl felt the desire to reach out her hands and place them on the child's knobby knees. She held her hands out just above the child's knees, thinking about touching them.

The girl tilted her head.

Cheryl bit her lip. "How about this? I'll ask you a question, and you can answer by nodding your head yes or shaking it for no? You can do that, can't you?"

The girl nodded, and Cheryl's heart grew light with hope.

"Okay. Good. You've already done one. It's easy." Cheryl looked at the bedroom doorway, expecting to see Adam there at any moment. When she didn't, she turned her attention back to the girl. She had to figure out how to get as much information as possible from her using simple yes or no questions. "You like this house. Did you live here once?"

The girl shook her head without giving the question much thought.

Adam appeared in the doorway. "How's it going? Is she still here?"

"I'm just trying to find some things out." She looked back at the girl who was still staring straight into her eyes. "Did something bad happen here?"

The girl broke eye contact and looked over at Adam. When she returned her gaze to Cheryl, there was fear in her eyes that Cheryl had not seen before.

"Did someone hurt you?"

The girl hugged her teddy bear to her chest and looked off to the side, avoiding Cheryl's gaze.

"Is that why you're here? You're here because someone hurt you?" Cheryl watched the girl carefully.

Her eye twitched. She blinked rapidly, and a tear spilled out and rolled down her chubby cheek.

Cheryl took that to be a yes. "Who hurt you? What did they do to you?"

The girl blinked at her blankly.

"Okay. Yes or no questions. I forgot." Cheryl glanced over at Adam.

He kept looking back up the hallway. "We need to get Stephanie to the hospital. She doesn't look good."

Cheryl knew he was right, but the girl being here and actually interacting with her was an opportunity that she couldn't miss. What if the girl held the clue to solving this case? What if she could let her know how to get everything back to normal? She hated the idea of being alone in the house, but she also knew Stephanie needed immediate attention. "Why don't you take Stephanie to the hospital, and I'll stay here? That way I can get to know--" She looked at the girl who still stared at her with a flat expression. "I wish I knew your name."

The girl parted her lips. "Iris," she said so softly that Cheryl almost didn't hear.

Cheryl smiled. She was finally getting somewhere. "Iris." She turned to look at Adam. "Did you hear that? Her name is Iris."

He raised both his eyebrows. "I didn't hear anything." He looked down the hallway again.

"Anyway, how about you take Stephanie to the hospital, and I'll stay here with Iris. We'll talk and get to know each other. If Will shows up, I'll be here to make sure he's okay."

Adam wrinkled his forehead and drew in some air through his clenched teeth. "I don't like the idea of splitting up."

Stephanie groaned in the living room.

"Are you okay?" Adam called down the hall.

Cheryl immediately saw everything wrong with this picture. Stephanie was her best friend. She should be the one attending to her now, but she was the only one who could stay here and talk to Iris. Even though it felt like she was abandoning her friend, she knew that staying would help the most in the long run. "It's the best solution."

Adam sighed. "I know, but that doesn't mean I have to like it."

"I'll find a charger and plug in my phone, so you can call me." Even though Cheryl didn't want to take her eyes off Iris, she remembered why she had initially gone to the bedroom. She got up and went over to the dresser to pull out some comfortable clothes for Stephanie, a pair of leggings and an oversized T-shirt. "Stay here with Iris and keep an eye on her. I'll go get Stephanie dressed and tell her what's going on."

Adam held out his hand and frowned. "How do I keep an eye on someone I can't see?"

Cheryl rolled her eyes. "Stay here." She pointed at Iris. "You too, Iris. Stay here. I'll be right back."

Stephanie sat scrunched up in the far corner of the living room with the throw Cheryl had given her earlier pulled up beneath her chin. Long scrapes ran up her shinbones, exposing the pink flesh beneath the skin. Sticks and leaves were tangled in her dark brown hair. Cheryl approached her slowly like she would approach a wild animal.

"I got some clothes for you. You can put these on, and then Adam's going to take you to the hospital," she whispered.

Stephanie looked up at her with large round eyes. Cheryl

had never seen her look so frightened. What could've happened to her in the woods?

She held out the clothes and was surprised when Stephanie reached out and took them. Before that moment, she had seemed completely out of it. Cheryl had wondered if she was even aware that they were speaking to her. She was aware. She heard everything she said.

"Do you need help putting them on?" Cheryl crossed her arms over her chest. Seeing her friend look so injured and vulnerable made her feel vulnerable too. She knew that feeling. She felt it before, the type of animal fear that seems to take humanity from you.

Stephanie shook her head and slowly began to stand.

Cheryl turned around to give her friend privacy but not before noticing the bruises crisscrossing her thighs like she'd been tied up with rope. "Were you in the woods all this time? Adam and I were just there, and it was starting to get dark. I was terrified. I can't imagine spending the whole night out there alone. When Will called and said that--" She knew she shouldn't tell Stephanie about Will now, but she would have to tell her eventually. Cheryl pursed her lips. Hopefully, he would come back, and she would have to tell Stephanie anything. "When Will called and said you were gone, I was so scared." After she'd already spoken, she realized that telling Stephanie about how scared she was when Stephanie was sitting here obviously terrified was kind of ridiculous. "Anyway, I'm glad you're back. No matter what happened, we're going to take care of it." When she stopped hearing motion behind her, she assumed that Stephanie was dressed and turned around. Stephanie stood in front of the sliding glass doors with her shoulders slumped. "Wait here. I'll get Adam. He'll take you to the hospital. I can't go with you because I have something to take care of here, but you'll be okay with Adam. You know that."

Stephanie chewed on her thumbnail, and she looked at the floor.

Cheryl rushed over to her and hugged her. She held on to her for a long time, emotion swelling in her chest. "I was so scared I would never see you again. I can't tell you how glad I am that you're back." Her voice cracked.

When she noticed that Stephanie was not hugging her back, she let go. She looked at her longtime friend's face, so familiar and so strange all at once.

"Anyway, I'll go get Adam." She patted her shoulder before turning to walk away.

Chapter 16

Stephanie sat in the backseat with her legs drawn up to her chest. Pressing her knees to her eyes, she shook ever so slightly. Adam thought she was crying, but he couldn't see her face, so he didn't know for sure.

He checked on her in the rearview mirror. "We're almost there."

His phone rang, and he looked at the screen to see who it was. "I have to get this. It's Day." He spoke to her like she was a child because he didn't know what else to do. He looked in the rear mirror at her one last time before answering the phone. "Hi, Day. You'll never guess what happened to us."

"I'm so glad to hear your voice. After I lost Cheryl, I was worried sick. I just tried to call her, and it went straight to voicemail." Day's voice was crisp and clear.

"She's supposed to be finding a charger for her phone." Adam was watching for the hospital. He knew they were getting close and hoped to see signs reassuring him that he was going in the right direction.

"You're not still in the woods then. Are you together?" There was a hint of concern in her voice.

"We found our way out just after dark. Stephanie turned up--"

"She did? That's amazing." Day interrupted. "I'm so glad."

"She's in the car with me now. I'm taking her to the hospital." Adam took a right, and as soon as he did, he saw a hospital sign pointing straight ahead.

"The hospital? Is she hurt?"

He looked in the rearview mirror again. She hadn't moved. "She has some minor scrapes and bruises, but she's not talking. Something terrible must've happened to her." The red and white emergency room sign glowed in the distance.

"So you have no idea what happened to her besides what's on the video?"

"Cheryl told you about the video?" Their time in the woods had been so stressful that he didn't remember Cheryl mentioning the video to Day on the phone, but then again, she was far behind him at points. They were getting closer to the hospital now, and Adam knew he would have to end the call. "Is something up?"

Day paused for a minute. He heard something on the other end, clicking like she was typing. "I don't know if this is helpful, but I found this article about a little girl who disappeared in the nature preserve. Her name was Iris McAdams. There's a picture of her in the article, and she looks like the little girl Stephanie said she saw. I'm emailing it to Cheryl now."

"Did you say her name was Iris?"

"Yeah, Iris McAdams. I've just been searching for all kinds of articles about the area. I feel like I'm on a bit of a wild goose chase. I don't know what I'm looking for exactly." More tapping sounds came over the line. "There are so many strange things. I have a list of people who've disappeared in the preserve."

"And these disappearances are recent?" he asked.

"Some are. The more current ones tend to be children who wandered off by themselves when they were out with their families."

Adam thought about Will again. They left him out there. "So this Iris McAdams, when did she disappear?"

"She disappeared about two years ago yesterday. That's a coincidence." She paused. "Okay, maybe it's not. Ghosts like to show up on anniversaries, don't they?"

"You know more about that than I do." Adam always appreciated the way Day acted like all this was normal. It probably was for her because she had been working with the supernatural for longer than he had. "Cheryl is back at the house with her now. If she's a missing child, all this should be pretty straight forward, right?" He knew that much of what Cheryl did was talk to the ghosts and help them find closure. If that was all this child needed, surely Cheryl could help. Maybe getting her to cross over would be as simple as telling her parents what happened to her.

"That depends. Working with ghosts is never that simple." It was not the answer that Adam wanted.

Only a few cars sat in the hospital parking lot. He hoped the emergency room wasn't busy. "I'm at the hospital now."

"Okay. Call me when you know something."

"I will." He pulled into a parking spot near the door. "Bye." He hung up. "We're here." He turned off the car, but when he looked in the rearview mirror, he couldn't believe what   he   saw.

**

Cheryl sat on the floor in front of Iris, who hadn't moved from her spot sitting on the end of the bed since she showed up that night. Cheryl couldn't help but think about Stephanie and Adam, hoping they got to the hospital okay. She hadn't had any luck finding a charger and held her dead cell phone in her hand as she sat cross-legged on the floor.

"Iris is a pretty name."

The girl looked down at the teddy bear in her lap.

"Do you have a last name?"

The girl nodded slowly.

Cheryl didn't say anything else. If she had patience, maybe the girl would tell her. She waited for a few minutes, which felt like an eternity.

The girl tugged at her teddy bear's arm.

When Cheryl finally gave up on getting an answer, she said, "That's okay, Iris. You don't have to tell me your last name right now. But I want you to know that we're friends, and friends tell each other lots of things. You can tell me anything. Okay?" Cheryl nervously chewed on the inside of her cheek as she waited for an answer.

After thinking for a few moments, Iris nodded.

"Good."

Cheryl thought she saw a hint of a smile on Iris's face.

"Why do you like coming to this house? Did you used to live here?"

Iris blinked.

"Sometimes, I like to go back to the places I used to live in." She looked at Iris's face, her chubby cheeks, and large dark eyes. "Is that why you come here?"

Iris shook her head. "Okay." She wasn't getting much, but at least she was getting some answers from her. Cheryl just had to figure out the right questions to ask. "Do you come here because something bad happened here?"

The muscles in Iris's face tensed. She lifted her teddy bear to her chest and hugged it.

"Iris, you can tell me what happened to you. I'm here to help, but I can't help you if I don't know what I'm helping you with." She was so close to finding something out. She could feel it. This was the part Cheryl loved. If she could truly help Iris that would make everything worth it.

Iris closed her eyes, and her eyelids fluttered.

"I know it's hard." Cheryl wanted to be able to reach out and touch her so badly. She wanted to comfort her. "It's okay to tell me. If you tell me, I can help you make it all better."

Iris opened her large eyes.

"Are you going to tell me?" Cheryl asked.

Iris leaned forward, reaching out for Cheryl. Her tiny hand plunged into Cheryl's chest, sending Cheryl falling to the floor.

**

Stephanie was in a house, her house. Then she was in a car, not her car. On some level, she knew that. She remembered dressing and Cheryl speaking to her, hugging her. She remembered walking through her front yard and climbing into the back seat of a car that smelled brand new, but what had happened before all of that? Why did she feel like she was floating through these moments? Why did she feel like she was on the edge of being completely out of control?

Maybe the truth was that she didn't want to remember because what she'd seen was too terrible. She let her thoughts explore that idea for only a few minutes before deciding that avenue was too dangerous to travel.

There was a woman whose face was made of bugs. When Stephanie saw her, she shivered with fright, but the woman kept her from running. Stephanie wasn't sure how, but she knew that the woman with the crawling face had captured her mind.

She told Stephanie that she was trying to keep her safe.

That couldn't be true. Stephanie didn't feel safe. She felt the opposite of safe. Even now that the woman was no longer with her and she sat in a car with Adam, she felt distinctly unsafe.

Adam talked. He talked a lot as he drove. Stephanie was too panicked to pay attention to what he said. His voice became a series of sounds playing in the background of her thoughts.

Being friends with Cheryl was funny, especially since she started this new business. She told Stephanie all kinds of things that Stephanie only half believed. Monsters, ghosts, demons, possession, they only happened in movies, not in someone's normal life. Stephanie went to an office every weekday. She did her best at work. She was engaged. She'd bought her dream house. This wasn't the kind of thing that happened to someone like her, except now it was.

**

Adam turned around in the front seat to look at Stephanie. He had expected to see her sitting with her knees pulled up to her chest and her head tucked in like she was trying to make herself into a neat little ball. That was the way she had been sitting for the entire drive, but this time she sat upright in the seat. Her feet were on the floor, and her back was perfectly straight. She looked right at Adam with eyes rimmed in red from crying. She was still, very still. Adam would've been very still too because in her lap sat an opossum. The scruffy furred creature blinked a few times at Adam before opening its mouth to show off a row of impressively sharp teeth.

"Where did that come from?" There was no way an

opossum the size of a large house cat could have gotten into the car without him knowing.

Stephanie didn't answer. Adam didn't expect her to.

"Don't panic. Just stay still." He got out of the car, leaving the driver side door open. He was already running through a mental list of what he knew he had in the trunk, which was not much of anything.

He decided that he would have to open the back door and hope the opossum would run out. Maybe he could open both back doors and scare the critter from one door into running out of the car through the other. It sounded like a good plan. He knew he would have to pull it off without Stephanie's assistance.

He opened the passenger side door that was closest to Stephanie and explained the plan to her even though she didn't seem to hear him or even register his existence. When she continued staring straight ahead, he didn't even bother finishing his explanation. He stood holding the back door open and looking at Stephanie's profile.

The opossum hissed, drawing Adam's gaze down to it. Its pink tail looped around Stephanie's wrist. It opened its mouth, and this time instead of hissing, it spoke.

"Don't trust him," the low rumble of a voice said.

Adam nearly slammed the car door shut and walked away. Animals were talking to him now. Had he been drugged? He took a deep breath. "Did you just say something?" What a ludicrous thing this was to say to an opossum!

"Don't trust him." Drool dripped from the corner of the opossum's mouth.

Adam laughed long and hard. He bent over and held his stomach in an exaggerated display of hilarity. He could deal with ghosts and demons. He was okay with the idea of different dimensions. He was okay with the idea of traveling into parallel worlds, but a talking opossum was where he drew the line. What was his life becoming? How was any of this happening? Maybe he needed to be admitted to the emergency room too. They could put him in the psych ward. He could imagine himself in a rubber room wearing a straitjacket. He laughed again, knowing that if his sister had seen him, she would tell him that wasn't funny. Their grandmother was mentally ill, and even though Adam didn't remember it because he was too young, his sister still remembered going to the hospital to see her. Maybe it ran in the family. Adam hadn't even considered it until now.

He took a few deep breaths trying to calm himself down. "Okay. You talk now." He looked around the parking lot to see if anyone could see him. "I'd appreciate it if you got out of my car."

The opossum looked at him with its shiny black eyes. It yawned but didn't move.

"All right then. You heard my plan already, so I'm going to execute it now." Adam walked around to the other side of the car to open the other door. When he got there, he whipped the back door open only to find the opossum was gone. Stephanie still sat perfectly straight in the backseat of the car.

"Where did it go?" he asked, momentarily forgetting that Stephanie wasn't talking.

Stephanie turned her head and looked at him. It was the first time since she'd returned that he saw a spark of life in her eyes. She had acknowledged his existence instead of staring straight through him.

"That was freaky, but I bet you've seen even stranger things where you've been."

She nodded slowly.

He felt like he had finally broken through. "Come to think of it, I've seen stranger things too. A little talking opossum is nothing."

She smiled. It wasn't a big smile, but it was enough of a smile to make Adam happy.

"Let's get you inside and have a doctor check you out. We need to make sure you're okay." He held out his hand to her and helped her out of the car.

Chapter 17

Iris cried and cried.

"Just let her wear the dress so that we can get going." Her father stood in the doorway of her bedroom, dressed in khaki shorts and a T-shirt. "She'll be miserable. Then she won't do this again."

Her mother scowled. "She's not the only one who will be miserable. I'll have to listen to her complain, and the dress will be ruined by the end of the day." She held up a pair of shorts in front of Iris. "Here, honey. You need to put this on to go hiking."

Iris crossed her arms over her chest and poked out her bottom lip. "No! I want to wear this." She didn't understand what the big deal was. Her mother had told her she could start picking out her own clothes, and she liked her red dress. She wanted everyone to see her in it at the park. Maybe she would see some fairies there, and they would think she was a princess. She wished she really could be a princess. She didn't know why some girls got to be princesses, and others didn't.

"Okay," her mother said. She let out a puff of air in exasperation. "You can wear your red dress, but you have to keep up. No complaining when you get too hot. No crying if your feet hurt." She looked down at the patent leather Mary Janes Iris had already put on all by herself.

Iris nodded her head.

When her parents told her she was going to a park, she pictured a swing set and a jungle gym, but this wasn't the kind of park where you meet lots of friends and go down the slide. This park was all trees and grass and dragonflies that zoomed through the air. They walked up trails that cut through the trees. Iris's shiny black shoes pinched her feet, but she didn't complain. Instead, she fell behind. While her father and her older brother ran ahead, Iris walked stiff-legged in an attempt to nurse her aching feet. Her mother stopped every few minutes to take pictures.

"The light is amazing. Look at how green the leaves are." She pointed her phone up into the canopy and snapped pictures.

The park was beautiful. It was precisely the kind of place Iris imagined fairy princesses lived. She scanned the trees off the path, looking for holes in their trunks that could lead to a whole other fairy world.

Her father and brother were way ahead, and her mother was taking pictures of the gnarled branches of an oak tree when Iris noticed something glint back in the trees. She swore she had heard a bell ring and thought for sure it was a fairy calling her. She walked over and tapped her mother, pointing at the flash of light breaking through the dimness of the thick forest.

"Look!" she said.

Her mother waved her away. "In a minute."

Meanwhile, the fairies were getting away. The light kept getting smaller, and the sound of the bell faded in the distance. Iris couldn't wait for her mother. She had to go now if she was going to enter fairyland. So she went. Ignoring her sore feet, she ran into the trees. She ran to the light, imagining how happy she would be when the fairies greeted her. She would eat tiny pieces of cake with them, and maybe they would teach her to fly.

There were no fairies at the light. There was only a man, a very bad man.

Some things are too terrible to remember, so Iris kept them tucked away. She remembered the park and her parents and her brother because that was the last time she saw them. She remembered the light and the bell because she had hoped so much that they were fairies. She wasn't sure why she still remembered the bad man's face, broad and sharp like someone on television. He smiled stiffly, and fear coursed through her. She didn't remember anything after that until she woke up in the bug woman's arms. She screamed when she first saw her face crawling with all the insects. Iris was afraid to touch her, but when she tried to run away, she saw a horde of animals surrounding them. Baring their teeth, they snarled at her. Iris shook with terror. She looked up at the woman who had millipedes as lips and white leaf notcher bugs as teeth and pleaded with her. "Please let me go. My parents are looking for me." She imagined her mother turning around and around on the trail, calling her name. She imagined her father and her brother running through the woods looking for her. She hoped they wouldn't be too angry with her when they finally found her.

"This is your family now." The bug woman gestured to the animals. When she spoke, her voice was a chorus of different voices all talking together. "You live with us now."

Iris cried out. "No!" She shot up, trying to run through the circle of animals, but something caught hold of her leg, and she tripped and fell. She looked down to see a vine wrapped around her ankle.

"You can't go home now. You can never go home." The woman stood and helped Iris to her feet. The vine around her leg unwound itself. "Come with me."

Iris didn't intend to follow the bug woman. She ground her feet into the dirt, prepared to stay put. If the bug woman didn't let her go back to her family, she would stand there until her family found her. She stood firm, imagining she was a tree that couldn't be moved. She pictured tree roots running from the soles of her feet into the ground, but she was small, and, though stubborn, the power of her mind was no match for the bug woman who lifted her up and carried her.

Iris fought kicking and screaming, but the bug woman ignored her. Iris swung her hands, trying to strike the woman in the face, but each time her hand plunged into her, creeping insects encased her fist. None of her blows affected the woman, who continued walking forward at a slow and steady pace until she reached a large oak tree with a crooked trunk. There she dropped Iris to the ground. She landed with a jolt, pain shooting up her back. She cried out before flipping over and attempting to run. After only a few steps, she fell, and this time came face-to-face with a girl that looked just like her. She had the same large eyes. Her hair was cut in the same way, a bob with bangs straight across her forehead. This girl wasn't moving. She lay in the grass with her head turned to one side. Her eyes were closed, and her hands were folded neatly atop her chest. She wore the same red dress Iris wore. She was missing a shoe. A mixture of dirt and blood was packed beneath her toenails. At first, Iris didn't understand. How was she looking at herself?

"Who is that?" She stood up and pointed at the sleeping girl on the ground who looked like her.

"You," the bug woman said.

Even though Iris tried not to understand what she saw, deep inside, she knew. She had learned about dying when her grandfather died. They had all dressed in black and gone to the funeral. Iris went too, even though at first her father said she was too young. Last year her guinea pig died. He had nested himself into a corner, his abdomen rising and falling rapidly. He didn't move for some time until finally, every ounce of life seeped out of him. They had a funeral for him like the one for her grandfather, except they buried him in the backyard beneath the mango tree. Iris used popsicle sticks to make the tombstone. When the bug woman told her that she was dead, she knew what that meant. She stood over her body and looked at it with curiosity. Then she looked back to the bug woman who looked at her through eyes that were gaping black holes.

Sensing her sadness, the bug woman plunged her arm into the dirt and pulled up a stuffed animal packed with mud. She struck it on the ground a few times, and the dirt fell away, revealing a worn bear with one eye missing and the stitching coming undone. She held it out to Iris. It wasn't like Iris's other toys, the ones she had in the home that she would never be allowed to go back to. The bear was old and threadbare and smelled like wet earth, but it was something to hold onto, so she took it. She wrapped her arms around it and squeezed it into her chest.

"Let's go," the bug lady said. "He'll be back to bury you soon just like he's buried the others."

Iris still couldn't explain why she followed the bug woman back further into the woods. After seeing all she'd seen, she felt like that was the only place she belonged. Maybe there was no fairyland after all. Maybe there never was. Or maybe the fairies would be waiting for her once she told everyone about what   the   bad   man   did.

**

Cheryl opened her eyes with a start. She lay on her back on the floor. At first, she had no idea where she was. The final remains of bluish light trickled in through a window. There was a soft carpet beneath her back. She sat up and looked around and realized she was in Stephanie and Will's bedroom. Everything that had just happened to her came flooding back. The girl's memories became her memories, but the girl in the red dress was gone. "Iris!" she called. She listened and only heard silence.

Adam had taken Stephanie to the hospital. She remembered that now, but that must've happened ages ago. Sitting up, she noticed her phone on the bed. She reached over for it. The battery was dead. Cheryl's thoughts whirled as she stood. She needed to find out where Stephanie and Adam were, but she was still a bit unsteady on her feet. She stumbled toward the bedroom door, gripping the doorjamb to steady herself. She heard the front door open.

"Adam? Stephanie?" She hurried down the hallway, and when she got there, Adam and Stephanie were not there to greet her.

**

After a few hours, Stephanie started looking better. The emergency room doctor examined her thoroughly and only found minor injuries. After the doctor left and they were finally alone, surrounded by the mint and white curtains that separated her bed from the others in the large room, she finally started talking.

"They showed me things in the woods." A tear ran down her face, and she pushed it away with her hand. "I was wrong about everything. I don't know how I could've been so wrong."

Adam had no idea what she was talking about, but the distress in her voice set him on edge. He took hold of her hand and squeezed it.

"I thought I was so perceptive."

A nurse dressed in green scrubs pulled back the curtain before he could ask Stephanie what she meant. Adam looked at his phone and wondered if the police would ever show up. They didn't. No one came to interview her at the hospital.

When they left, Stephanie shuffled through the parking lot to the car, her flip flops scrapping the asphalt as she went. She crossed her arms over her chest and looked at the ground as she walked.

"What did you mean by what you said inside?" Adam asked as he opened the passenger-side door for her.

She sighed. "Let's get going. I'll tell you in the car."

She waited until they pulled out of the hospital parking lot before she started to tell Adam her story.

**

Stephanie had no idea how she would tell anyone what she had just experienced. She knew it would sound crazy, so she wanted to wait to tell Cheryl first. If anyone would understand, Cheryl would, but she wasn't with Cheryl. Adam had asked, and knowing what she knew about Adam, she thought he would probably believe her, even though she didn't believe herself.

She half expected him to accuse her of seeing things. He didn't. When she described the bug lady to him, he knew what she was talking about even though he hadn't seen it himself. He knew about the animals in the forest and the way the trees seemed to come to life. The fact that he wasn't shocked made her wonder if she was telling the story correctly.

It wasn't until she described what the bug woman had shown her that Adam sat up in his seat and looked over at her.

"Are you sure?" he asked, questioning her for the first time.

"I saw it with my own eyes." She didn't know. She was shown it, and even while claiming it was the truth, she wondered if she could trust her claims. Could she trust anything? Was her mind playing tricks on her? But no matter how fantastic it sounded, it all seemed so real.

"We should call the police." She had no idea how she'd explain this to the police, but it was the right thing to do.

"We already have." Adam looked over at her with wide eyes. "Will's missing. He went into the woods and never came back."

Chapter 18

"Will." Cheryl swallowed a lump that suddenly formed in her throat. "What happened? We looked all over for you in the woods."

Will slammed the door and turned the deadbolt. Panting, he rushed into the kitchen, pulled a glass from the cupboard, and filled it with water. He gulped it down, drips of water falling from the corners of his mouth onto his dirt-streaked shirt.

Cheryl turned on the light in the kitchen.

Will squinted and turned to look at her.

There were wounds on his hands that looked like bite marks and a purple bruise high on his cheek. Cheryl stood, staring at him, not sure what to do next. She hated that her phone was dead and she couldn't get into a car and drive away. When would Adam and Stephanie get back? What was she supposed to do until then?

The mere thought of being alone with Will for even a moment longer turned her stomach. She tried to keep her breathing steady and calm. "Stephanie came back."

That caught his attention. He leveled his gaze at her and put the glass on the counter. "Where is she?" He rushed through the kitchen toward the hallway.

"She's not here. Adam took her to the hospital." He stopped dead in his tracks and spun around. "Was she hurt?"

Knowing what she knew, she couldn't see anything he did the same anymore. She wondered if he really was concerned or acting. He was such a good actor. "I don't know. They've been gone for ages. We stayed out there looking for you. We ran around in the woods until it got dark. When we got back to the house, she was already here, sitting right there." She pointed to the corner in the living room near the sliding glass door.

Will rushed into the room to see where she was pointing. "What happened to her?"

There were so many questions Cheryl wanted to ask, but she didn't because bringing any of them up might put her life in danger. "She looked pretty banged up. I think she was in shock. She wouldn't say anything. Adam took her to the hospital, and I was supposed to stay here to--" She suddenly realized that she probably shouldn't mention Iris. "I was supposed to stay here to wait to see if you showed up, and here you are." The last bit sounded more enthusiastic than she intended.

He narrowed his eyes at her, and Cheryl wondered if he could see the fear in her. "Thank you." His voice softened. "I always thought you didn't like me."

Cheryl shifted her gaze. Why was he bringing this up now? "That's not true. I'm glad Stephanie has found someone. She deserves to settle down. God knows she's wanted to for ages." Cheryl's throat tightened as she told her lie.

He raked his fingers through his hair, pulling out a couple of leaves and tossing them to the floor. They stood there for a few moments looking at each other and saying nothing.

Cheryl realized that all she needed to do was stay calm and wait till Stephanie and Adam returned. "What happened to you out there? You looked pretty freaked out when you came in."

He squeezed his eyes closed and shook his head like he was trying to shake something off. "You wouldn't believe me if I told you."

She turned on the living room light and sat down on the sofa. She leaned forward, resting her chin on her hand. "Try me."

He looked at the door. "Maybe we should go to the hospital to see if Stephanie's okay." He looked at her for a moment like he was trying to see into her. "Stephanie didn't tell you anything."

Cheryl shook her head. "No. Should she have?" She looked at the clock on the cable box beneath the TV. "They might have already left. My phone's dead, but you can try to call Adam."

"He pulled his phone from his pocket. "My battery is almost gone too." He scrolled through his numbers. "I don't have his number."

Cheryl glanced over at the end table, where Stephanie's phone sat. "I don't know it. Nobody memorizes phone numbers anymore. Too bad Stephanie's phone is here." The feeling of dread that she usually had outside of the house was thick in the air now. Bile bubbled up in her stomach, and she kept having to swallow to keep from vomiting. She was sitting on a sofa, talking casually about phone numbers with a monster. This was how she was going to stay alive.

"What's that?" He pointed to the corner of the room where Stephanie had been sitting when Adam and Cheryl came home. A tiny scuffed black Mary Jane shoe sat on the floor. "How did that get there?"

He went over and snatched the shoe up in his hand. He let it dangle from his index finger as he looked at it with disgust. "I don't know." She wanted to run out the door and into the street, yelling for the police, but that wouldn't work.

He narrowed his eyes at her. "Where did you get this? Have you been going through my things?"

Cheryl looked at the shoe swaying casually back and forth on his index finger. She thought about Iris in the park in her party dress, and her blood ran cold. "What if I had? Shouldn't I be the one questioning why a grown man has a missing girl's shoe hidden away?"

His nostrils flared. "I don't know what kind of game you're playing. You think you can scare me. You never really wanted Stephanie to be happy. You're jealous."

She laughed. She couldn't help herself. The idea was so preposterous. "Jealous? Why would I be jealous that my best friend is engaged to a perverted murderer like you?"

"Murderer?"

Time stood still for a few seconds as she watched his face harden. Cheryl's heart rose into her throat.

He hurled the shoe at her. "This was you all along. I don't know how you knew. I don't care. It doesn't matter now." His face twisted with anger, and he lunged at her. His hands were around her neck before Cheryl could think of what to do. If she had been standing up, she would have been able to defend herself, but sitting like she was with one leg tucked beneath her made it hard to fight him. She punched him as hard as she could, but her blows had little effect. If only she could kick him. She was good at kicking.

He squeezed her neck, pressing her windpipe closed. She reached up, grabbing at his wrists as her cells used their last bits of oxygen. Her eyes bulged. His angry red face hovered above hers. The world around her began to spin, and her peripheral vision went black. Will's angry face was all she could   see.

**

Stephanie looked out the car window into the darkness. Tears streaked down her cheeks. She didn't know what to believe anymore. Her anger and disgust mixed with embarrassment. "I got up in the middle of the night because I thought I heard something in the house. But as soon as I got up, I felt like I was moving around on autopilot." She tucked a strand of hair behind her ear and looked over at Adam. She didn't want to tell him, but she had to. "It was like someone had taken over my body, and I was aware, but I couldn't control what I was doing. I knew I was leaving the house and walking into the yard, but I couldn't stop myself. Then the fence just seemed to melt away in front of me, and I walked into the forest. I don't know how long I walked. Sharp stones and twigs jabbed into the soles of my feet. I felt the pain but couldn't stop. I just kept going." She paused.

Adam looked over at her briefly with pity on his face. "What happened next?"

She swallowed. "I was pretty far out where the trees are really dense when I saw someone in the distance. It looked like Will, so I waved my arms and tried to yell at him, but I couldn't. I still didn't have control. I stopped walking and crouched down behind a bush and watched." She gasped and began to cry. "What I saw was so awful. I still can't believe it's true." She sniffled and wiped the tears from her eyes, taking a few moments to compose herself. "Will was with the little girl, the one I keep seeing in the red dress. He was crouched down, talking to her. Then he hit her, and she fell to the ground." Stephanie gasped and covered her mouth. Tears flowed down her face. "He grabbed her by the neck and lifted her up against a tree, choking her. She kicked her legs and grabbed at his arms, trying to get free. I couldn't believe what I was seeing." Her throat tightened, and all the air left her lungs as she replayed the scene in her mind. She leaned over, resting her elbows on her knees and her head on the dashboard. "I wanted to jump up. I wanted to stop him. I wanted to save that little girl, but I couldn't move. I kept trying, and somehow I must have broken whatever spell I was under because I ran at them. When I reached them, they had disappeared into nothing. It was like a mirage. They weren't really there, but I was finally free. So I kept on running. Or at least I tried to, but the trees seemed to come alive around me, and I fell. Vines wrapped themselves around me, holding me still." Her voice quivered, and she sniffled. "That's when I saw the bug woman. Do you think I'm crazy?"

Adam shook his head. "Not at all."

"Just thinking about her makes my skin crawl. She came close to me and touched me. That's when I saw--" She began to sob violently, her whole body shaking uncontrollably. She put her face in her hands. She wanted all of this to be over.

"What did you see?" Adam's voice was calm and measured.

Her breath hitched. "I saw him over and over again doing what he did to that little girl to other children. I saw him in the woods, burying them." She looked at Adam, trying to measure his response.

"So you're telling me that Will is a serial child murderer?"

"Yes, I guess I am." The words sunk in. "I thought I knew him, but I didn't know anything. I don't understand how this could happen?"

Adam stepped on the accelerator. "We have to get to your house. Cheryl is there alone. What if he comes home?"

**

Cheryl didn't know why he let go of her neck, but she was

just thankful he did. She sucked in the air, coughing and wheezing. Scrambling out from under him, she looked up at his face now wide with fear. He was looking at something in the middle of the living room. Cheryl turned to see what it was and saw five children all about the same age standing there. The girl in the red dress stood in front of them, holding her shoe in the air.

"What's happening?" He reached down, grabbing hold of Cheryl's arm hard. "Do you see that? The shoe? It's just floating there." He looked over at her. "How are you doing that?"

Of course, he couldn't see what she was seeing, the children who must have been his victims. "I'm not--" Before Cheryl could finish her sentence, Will screamed.

"Oh my God, they're here. That's impossible. That's impossible."

The children laughed and pointed at him as if amused by his horror.

He charged to the middle of the living room, running through their ghostly forms. "What's happening?"

Swarms of bugs crawled out from beneath the furniture. Roaches, beetles, spiders, and millipedes scuttled out from the dark edges of the room. Their legs clacked against the tile as they scurried toward him. They poured through cracks in the walls, under appliances, and beneath the door into the middle of the room. Will's mouth hung open in horror as they crawled atop each other, finally taking the form of a woman. Upon seeing her, he turned to run to the front door. He tried to open it, but it wouldn't budge. He fumbled with the lock. It wouldn't turn. "Help!" He yelled. He looked back at Cheryl with wide eyes.

She could find no pity in her heart for him. The bug woman came toward him, her entire body moving like a wave.

He pulled at the door in desperation. The animals that swirled around her feet hissed and snarled. The opossum stood on her shoulders, his mouth open, showing his pointed teeth. "You will harm no more," the opossum said in a deep voice.

Will's face turned red. He grabbed hold of his chest and collapsed to the floor, making a gurgling sound as he fell. The opossum climbed down from the woman's shoulders and stood on his fallen body. His eyes were still open, but fear paralyzed him. "It is over." The opossum stood with his nose over Will's and inhaled deeply, seeming to suck the breath out of him. Will's breathing stopped. His body went limp. The opossum sauntered back over to the bug woman, crawling up her body to his resting place on her shoulders before they all disappeared.

Cheryl stood over Will's lifeless body. Her whole life was about death now, but that hadn't made witnessing it easy.

A car pulled up in the driveway. In the silence, she heard the engine outside and the tires on the driveway. A car door slammed. She took a deep breath, knowing that she'd have to explain all of this to Stephanie. She'd been through so much already. It pained her to be the one to ruin her best friend's dream of happily ever after.

Chapter 19

Adam called Cheryl's phone on the way back to the house. It was still off. His mind raced, imagining all the terrible things that could happen. He couldn't lose her, especially not like this. The tires skidded as he turned down Stephanie's street. Blind with fear, he nearly forgot Stephanie was in the car with him. He tore into the driveway, threw the car into park, and leaped out, leaving the keys in the ignition. When he got to the door and found it locked, panic swept through him.

He turned, seeing Stephanie getting out of the car and coming toward him. "Keys!" He yelled at her holding out his trembling hand.

"I don't--" Her words dropped away.

He raised his fist to bang on the door, and it swung open. Cheryl stood before him, her hair going every which way and her neck red. He pushed past her into the house. "It's him! Will killed the girl." There was no need for him to finish the story because Will lay lifeless in the middle of the living room floor.

Cheryl held her hand to her throat. "I know."

Stephanie came in before Adam had a chance to stop her. She stepped into the living room to see her fiancé's body motionless on the floor. She put her hand over her mouth and dropped to her knees before letting out a primal moan that welled up from someplace deep inside. Cheryl knelt beside her, wrapping her arms around her as she cried. "I'm sorry." She whispered between her sobs. "I didn't know."

Cheryl rubbed her back. "None of us knew."

**

The for-sale sign was already in the yard when Stephanie loaded the last of her belongings into her car. She slammed the trunk closed and stood in the driveway with her hands on her hips, looking at the house. She thought that the white Mediterranean with the red tile roof in a peaceful cul-de-sac was her dream house. She hoped that the square-faced man with the dimpled chin and anchorman's voice was her Prince Charming, who showed up to sweep her away. It turned out neither of those things was true. Even though her heart ached like a new bruise and her skin crawled at the thought of all what her life with Will had really been, she was ready to step into a new era of her life. She was a survivor. Iris and the bug woman taught her that she had the strength to move on no matter what Will had done.

She got into her car, slipped on her sunglasses, and eased her car out of the driveway. She pulled away, knowing that she was stepping into the future and would never look back again.

Chapter 20

They sat in the back corner of the coffee shop, away from prying ears. Day sipped her cappuccino. "Any new cases on the horizon?" She smirked at Cheryl.

"I'm glad to have a bit of a break," Adam said before taking a bite of his croissant.

"I never get a break." Cheryl watched the man in black walk toward her. The infectious beat of disco had announced his approach before he even appeared. His dark eyes focused on her as he walked in a straight line, through tables and chairs and other patrons to get to her.

"Are you okay?" Day watched her with recognition in her eyes. "Is a ghost here now?"

He was in no hurry to get to her. He walked with a calm swagger, his footsteps falling in time to the music.

Adam's cell phone rang. He pulled it from his pocket and answered it. "Suncoast paranormal."

Cheryl was only vaguely aware of him talking on the phone because she was giving her full attention to the ghost that stood before her now. He tapped his foot to the music. A dark stain seeped down the left leg of his tight jeans.

"What do you want? If you tell me what you need, I'll try to help you." Frustration tinged her words. Cheryl wanted a break, but the dead never seemed to rest.

As if responding to her question, the café dropped away,

and she found herself in the disco again. The music pulsated as the crowd danced in time like one living organism. The man in black turned away from her and walked into the crowd, bopping his head as he weaved his way between dancers. Cheryl rose from her chair and followed him. She saw the woman again in the gold stretch pants, her long black hair swaying back and forth as she danced. The man went around behind her and began to dance with her. Cheryl watched and waited, looking for a clue. What did he want her to do? All at once, the room plunged into darkness, and the music stopped. Cheryl froze. When the lights came on, everyone at the disco lay on the floor, their bodies draped across one another, motionless as if dead. Cheryl looked at the scene in horror. The music began to pump again, and she felt someone walking up behind her. She spun around to see the man in black, his face expressionless as he approached her. He extended his hand to her, and in his palm sat a pink and red mass of flesh. It took a moment for Cheryl to recognize what it was, a beating human heart. She yelped and stepped back.

"Come back to us. Are you okay?" Day held her by the shoulders and looked into her eyes.

Cheryl looked around to see that she was back in the café. People at their tables looked over at her. Some whispered to each other.

Bashfully, she held up her hand. "I'm sorry," she announced to the room. With her shoulders slumped, she went back over to their table just as Adam hung up his phone.

"Everything okay?" He looked from Day to Cheryl as if he hadn't noticed what had happened.

"Yeah. I just saw that ghost again." Cheryl pulled out a chair and sat down.

"The disco ghost?" He placed the phone down on the

table.

Cheryl nodded. "Who was on the phone?"

Adam grinned. "It looks like we have another case."

Cheryl's heart fluttered with anticipation. She was exhausted, but this whole paranormal investigation thing was really working. She was ready to dive into another case. She was willing to take as many cases as they could get while they could get them. It was the way she was able to give to the world. Suncoast Paranormal was what she was always meant to do.

Do you want more books by Lovelyn Bettison?

Visit her website for more.

https://www.lovelynbettison.com/

ABOUT THE AUTHOR

Lovelyn Bettison writes stories about things that go bump in the night. She lives in St. Petersburg, Florida with her husband, son, and dog. She loves getting letters in the mail, Thai food, and having conversations with strangers in coffee shops. Find out more about her on her website: lovelynbettison.com.

ORE BOOKS BY LOVELYN BETTISON

SUNCOAST PARANORMAL

The Psychic
Monster in the House
Lady in the Lake
Girl in the Woods

ISLE OF GODS SERIES

The Vision
The Escape
The Memory
The Revenge (Coming Soon)

The Haunting Series

The Haunting of Warren Manor (Coming Soon)